THAWED OUT

THE MERRY EVERYTHING SERIES
BOOK 4

JODI PAYNE
BA TORTUGA

Thawed Out

Edited by LC Hinson

Cover illustration by AJ Corza
http://www.seeingstatic.com/

ISBN: 978-1-963644-08-1

Published by Tygerseye Publishing, LLC
November, 2024
Printed in the USA

THAWED OUT

By Jodi Payne & BA Tortuga

Thawed Out is an opposites attract, second chance romance featuring an established couple on the edge of divorce, a ferocious snow storm, precocious children and a healthy dose of holiday magic.

Kiren knows there is a storm coming when he goes to the cabin to deliver divorce papers to his husband Flynn, but he doesn't plan to stay long. He hates that it's come to this, but they just can't seem to do anything without arguing anymore. When he finds Flynn looking so skinny and unhappy, he ends up staying to talk.

And maybe to try harder not to break up their family.

Flynn knows Kiren is just as tired as he is. They both work hard. They both take care of their two kids. He doesn't want to give up, but between his long hours and going to school, he always seems to be in trouble when gets home.

Before they know it, they're snowed in with nothing but time on their hands. The two of them decide that they don't want to be frozen in the worst time of their married life. But can they work together to find the balance they need to start again together?

THE MERRY EVERYTHING SERIES

Window Dressing

Cowboy Protection

Cowboys and Cupcakes

Thawed Out

These books in this series are stand-alone stories. Some of them contain MCs from our other books but you can absolutely read these without reading those.

To our wives.
Merry Christmas!

1

Kiren sat in his car at the bottom of the winding Cedar Road. He'd been idling for a bit, reading the road sign over and over and working up the nerve to keep going. He glanced at the envelope on the passenger seat again, then sighed and took the right-hand turn toward the cabin where he was meeting his husband.

His soon to be ex-husband.

It was hard to believe all their arguing and hurt feelings and drama had been reduced to just a few words on paper. The end of their marriage felt heavy as hell but didn't look like much.

He needed this over with. He was worn out. Emotionally, physically, just done. They needed to put this behind them and move on.

The road was bumpy, tree-lined, and narrow in spots, but in others it was wide and cut through open pastures with amazing views. Usually. Today it was cloudy and really cold, and the visibility was very low. The bumpy road was covered in packed snow. It never got steep enough that he needed chains or anything, but he was glad for his all-wheel drive.

He finally made it to the cabin and parked in the guest space where his parents parked when they visited. Flynn's truck, which they usually drove up here as a family, was parked out front.

He shut the engine off and took a breath, and then another. It wasn't the papers that had him anxious; it was seeing Flynn. The wild, mixed emotions of the divorce had become so confusing that it actually made his stomach ache.

Get in, get the signatures, get out. You've got this. Easy.

He took one more breath, dragged the envelope off the passenger's seat, then climbed out of the car.

The front door opened, Flynn's face ashen under his tan. He'd gotten damn near gaunt in the last year, and his flannel shirt and jeans drowned him. "Is everything all right with the kids?"

He sighed. In Flynn's defense—for all that Flynn didn't need defending—cell service was spotty up here even in good weather. "They're fine. I texted you." He waved the envelope. "Papers."

"Jesus." Flynn stared at him a second then turned to head back in the house. "I guess it's fitting."

Fitting? What the fuck did that mean?

He was going to be sorry he did this, wasn't he? He should have just waited for Flynn to come back from hibernating in the mountains or whatever the fuck he was doing up here alone and let the lawyers handle everything. Hell, he could have just sent a courier up here.

But no, the one thing Flynn was right about was that he could be a bit of control freak. He knew that much about himself. He needed this done, and the best way to make sure was to do it himself.

He snorted as he climbed the steps. Maybe that was what Flynn meant by fitting.

Touché.

Fuck.

He opened the screen door just after it slammed shut behind Flynn and went inside.

Flynn headed straight for the kitchen and the coffee pot, pulling out a second mug before filling them.

"Do you have a little cream?" Flynn hadn't gone far. The kitchen was tiny and open to the living space. "I'm not staying long."

"I do. No? You're going to have to wait for me to read everything, so you can drink a cup of coffee."

"Mhm." And they didn't have to talk while Flynn was reading. He took the mug from Flynn, trading it for the envelope and took a sip. Flynn made a good cup of coffee. "Take your time."

He wandered around with his mug, noting the tequila on the kitchen counter and the blanket and pillow on the couch. He stopped to look at the pictures hanging on the wall. A couple of them were family pictures from Flynn's grandfather, but most of them were of just two of them, or of Jasper and Cassidy when they were tiny.

Good memories.

God, he hated this.

Flynn's grandfather had willed him this cottage, and Flynn adored it.

It wasn't much—one bedroom, a huge front room, a kitchenette, and a bathroom with a tub filled from the cistern and a composting toilet. The electricity was solar, so it was a little touch and go, and the heat was a pellet stove, but it was remote, the deck was to die for, and it was the quietest place he'd ever been.

He'd always loved it here, but not today. Today it felt like hell on earth. There wasn't enough air in the place.

"I should—you want me to take a little walk?"

Flynn's eyebrow went up, lips tightening, and he could almost hear the snarling words that had to be zipping through the man's head. "Whatever turns you on, babe."

Well, fuck, He'd thought Flynn would appreciate the space, but now? Now, he needed it. "Uh-huh." He zipped his coat back up, picked up his coffee, and stomped out the back door into the cold.

It was really cold. He pulled his hood up and zipped his coat even higher. It was pretty out here though; the woods were snowy and it was still and quiet. His coffee was going to get cold fast out here, so he took a big sip.

The wind was beginning to blow, and the sun didn't want to filter down through the trees, not even a bit.

He thought about texting Mom or maybe Walt, just to get some sympathy, but he had no signal. Dammit.

He tried to check the weather too, but no luck there either; the wheel just spun and spun and nothing ever loaded. No matter, he'd be leaving shortly, and if he really needed to know, there was a radio in the cabin somewhere. He'd go back in soon. He wasn't sure he trusted Flynn not to leave him standing out here just for the amusement factor.

He'd probably do the same.

He stepped off the wide deck and walked along the path Flynn had shoveled like always. It went out into the woods a bit to a firepit and some log benches. It also went all the way around the cabin, which was great when the kids needed somewhere to run.

By the time he got back his fingers were pretty well

frozen, so he stomped the snow off his boots and stepped out of them as he came back inside.

"Mm. Warm in here."

"Yeah. It's chilly today. We have to talk about this. I'm not letting the kids go for half the summer."

But he had summers off. This kept them out of daycare for five weeks. "Wait. What? Why not? We definitely talked about this. I'm off in the summer."

"I'm not going without them for weeks at a time. I can't, and I'm not going to give in on it."

He understood; he wouldn't want to either, but it was practical. "Flynn, it just makes sense. It's not ideal, okay, I know, but I can be home. It will save us money, and we can plan vacations. It's only half the summer."

"Okay, then I want winter and spring break and all the school holidays."

Flynn was just being spiteful now. "Spring break, fine. The rest—you're out of your mind. We're trading off."

"So what? You get the babies for five weeks, and I get one in exchange?" Flynn shook his head. "How the fuck is that reasonable?"

"Because you do shift work, and you need to find childcare in the summer, and I don't. If we split the cost of summer care, we're saving money. Or doesn't money matter to you anymore?" Was it fair? Maybe not. But it was practical.

"Oh fuck you! You think I'm busting my fucking ass to get my physician's assistant's license for fun? I started this so you could keep your fucking dream job with the students!" That was the most fire he'd seen from Flynn in a year.

He used to love it when Flynn was passionate about something. But he lowered his tone because he couldn't take the yelling anymore and went back to the coffee maker without looking at Flynn. "Wow. Pardon me. I thought this license was something you wanted. My dream job happens to be the job I have; I didn't know I needed to apologize for that."

Flynn slapped one hand on the table, making the coffee cup jump and rattle. "Seriously? You're going to be all... I left the circuit because we wanted kids. I worked nights at the ER because of the money. I started school so that I could keep the salary and work days. I'm fucking *tired*, man!"

He jumped, startled enough by the sound that his heart was pounding, then turned and stared at Flynn, not bothering lower his voice this time. "Right. How could I forget that you're the only one who has sacrificed for our children? You're always reminding me! Meanwhile, I obviously have plenty of time, plenty of money, and am totally well rested! Lucky fucking me."

If he wasn't driving he'd grab that bottle of tequila.

"I know we took a hit on the money. It was for two motherfucking years. You couldn't have my back for two years?"

"I did have you back for two years, Flynn. Jesus Christ." He sighed and turned back to the coffee maker. "Fine. We'll share the summer. Just write in whatever you want, and I'll have the lawyers fix it. I can't... I just can't do this. I can't argue anymore." He was exhausted too. Just completely out of spoons. "Whatever you want."

"I want my fucking life back!" The coffee cup went flying, smashing on the floor as Flynn stormed out, the entire cabin shaking.

"Fuck." *Me too.*

He watched the coffee run across the floor and sighed. It would be a shame if it made it over to the little rug Flynn's grandmother made. He looked found a broom and a towel to clean up, then threw all the pieces in the garbage.

The divorce papers were still on the table, and he didn't touch them.

He lit a lantern, hating how dark it was, but it was the longest night of the year, so...

The door opened up, Flynn's arms filled with wood, his lips blue.

"Jesus. Are you okay? Put that down." Kiren grabbed the blanket off the back of the couch, helped Flynn put the wood in the holder, then sat him in a chair near the stove and wrapped the blanket around his shoulders. "I'll get you more coffee. Your fucking lips are blue."

It was a testament to how cold Flynn was that he didn't argue. He simply sat and shivered.

He brought a hot mug of coffee back and put it in Flynn's hands, not letting go in case Flynn had trouble holding onto it. "Sip slowly."

Flynn took a sip, and dammit, the tears that had frozen on Flynn's eyelashes thawed, shimmering before they fell.

He pretended he didn't notice, but he definitely had, and it made his chest ache. Through all of this bullshit he'd never figured out where they'd lost each other and become something unfixable. They used to finish each other's sentences, read each other's thoughts. Now he was lucky when Flynn threw a mug because at least that was something he could understand.

"Thanks for the drink." Flynn's voice was raw, rough as a cob. "Sorry for breaking the cup."

Like he cared about a coffee mug. "I'm sorry I sprung this on you. I did text, but I should have known better."

"I needed a break. I finished finals and needed somewhere the phone couldn't find me."

"I get it. I shouldn't have come. I'll take off as soon as you thaw out." He stood and peered out the window. He'd thought the darkness was due to the weather, but no, it was plain old night out there now. "Shit. It's really dark. Well, I'll be careful."

"What?" Flynn frowned and stood up. "No. No, you know those roads aren't safe in the dark, especially not without a four-wheel drive."

He did know that; he and Flynn had learned that the hard way about six months before Jasper was born. It was sweet that Flynn seemed so worried about him doing something stupid. He sighed. "Yeah. Crap."

Flynn stared at him for a long minute, then breathed deep. "Are the kids expecting you home? Do I need to get the sat phone?"

"I guess we should tell Mom I'm stuck for the night, yeah." That was going to open another can of worms, but she was going to have questions either way.

"No reason to worry everyone. Jasper worries."

Yeah, their six-year-old was absolutely anxiety boy, worrying about everything.

"I know. Sorry about this. It's obviously not the downtime you were looking for."

Flynn waved his words away. "It's fine. You need to be safe. Tomorrow you can run down the mountain and all."

He nodded. "I can take the couch." He'd head out in the morning and do what he should have done in the first place —let the lawyers handle this shit.

"I've been sleeping there, if you want the bed. I can't—I haven't been sleeping in the bedroom."

That was how he felt about the house, especially when the kids weren't there. "Sure. Okay." He assumed the stuff he'd left in the closet and the dresser were still here. He probably even had a toothbrush.

"There's soup if you want it. Bread." Flynn stood up, wandering over to where their—the—satellite phone was plugged in. "Call your mom. I'm going to warm this place up."

"Thanks." He took the phone from Flynn, ignoring the tingle where their fingers touched, and made the call. He had enough juice in his phone to read a book for a while so, when he was done, he'd just tuck himself in and leave Flynn alone for the evening.

He dialed and waited for the call to connect.

2

Flynn drank until he stopped crying, then he crashed, wrapped up in his blanket, trying not to dream.

He and Kiren had made love for the first time here.

They'd brought both the babies here together to play, to learn about the Rockies, about bears and elk and porcupines.

Everything had gone to hell, and he didn't know what to do about it.

Their separation, a couple of months of living apart, hadn't cooled things off at all, hadn't made anything better. All it had done was make him miss what they used to have even more.

He didn't understand how Kiren was acting so cool about this. The last month or so, Kiren had been focused on getting the divorce papers done and signed, but the man looked like hell, it was obvious by the dark circles under Kiren's eyes that this was hard on him too.

Of course, who knew what Kiren was thinking. He sure as shit didn't.

Flynn had thought that he was going to be happy getting

off the road, but he hated working nights, he hated the constant stress of the ER, hated being off-kilter with the rest of the world.

Schooling was supposed to fix it, but...

It hadn't. It had just made him tired, hysterical, and divorced.

The world swirled around him, and he was afraid he was going to puke, so he launched himself off the sofa, yanked the cabin door open—

And fell into a drift of snow that was up to his waist.

The wind swirled around, and he could hear it in the trees, the eerie whistling and the sound of creaking branches meant this wasn't stopping any time soon. He could barely see Kiren's SUV in the driveway. It was hard to tell how much snow had fallen overnight because it was still blowing around, but Kiren wasn't going to be able to get out in this. Not today.

Likely not tomorrow either.

"Goddamn it." His cock was wet and cold, and his nipples were like ice. He thanked God for abs and pulled himself up. "Fuck-a-doodle-doo."

At least they had snowmelt...

"I felt the cold, I thought maybe the stove had gone out. What the fuck is that?" Kiren grabbed his shoulders and pulled him back from the doorway. "Jesus Christ."

"I fell. It's—It's snow." Duh, Kiren knew it was fucking snow. He lived here.

"No, really?" Kiren slammed the door closed and chuckled, sounding for a minute like his old self. "I have to save you from hypothermia two days in a row? Sit. Blanket. I'll start coffee, dork."

"I cleaned the pot out and set it up last night. Just plop it on the stove."

"Old habits." Kiren put the pot on the stove, turned it on, then went to look out the window. "Fuck. I can't get out in this. Do you know when it's supposed to stop?"

"No. I haven't cranked up the radio, but I will." He stripped off his wet pants and pulled on some dry sweats, staying near the stove.

Kiren was wearing his favorite flannel pajamas—red and black checked bottoms and a warm long sleeved black top. They stayed up here in the closet and never left. It was the only place Kiren had ever worn them.

"No rush; it's not stopping any time soon." Kiren sighed and whispered, "Fuck."

"Sorry. I had no idea." Obviously. He wasn't going to be stuck with someone that hated him on purpose.

"It's not like I told you I was coming." Kiren paced from the stove to the window and back, checking on the coffee. "I didn't think I'd be staying more than an hour yesterday, and I didn't even look. Sorry."

"Well, we're not going anywhere. They won't plow for a few days, once it stops." And it was about to be Christmas.

"I know. I remember." Kiren sighed and poured them coffee, bringing his mug over before going back to add cream to his own. "Damn it."

He sat, because there literally wasn't anything else to do but stare at each other.

Kiren dug around in the kitchen. "How are you for groceries?"

"I have eggs, bread, lunch meat, bacon, spam, potatoes, tons of canned soup and milk, beer, potable water, coffee." He stayed up here a lot.

"How do you feel about breakfast? I haven't eaten since lunch yesterday."

"I could eat." Or barf. Or just have a meltdown. "I'll grab

the skillet. The stove is running high now." He didn't have to be worried about cooling the food at least.

Kiren nodded, handed him the bacon, then got the eggs out and started scrambling. How many times had they done this before?

How come it felt so fucking awful now?

They didn't talk as they made breakfast, and they didn't say a word while they ate either. Kiren wasn't stomping around, but he could see the tension in Kiren's forehead and feel it across the breakfast table. Kiren ate though; the man never had trouble eating no matter what was going on.

He picked at the food, eating enough that Kiren wouldn't fuss at him, but everything tasted like cardboard. Nothing was going to be right again. He knew it.

Kiren glanced at him more than once, and he knew he was being sized up. He'd lost weight, he looked tired, he wasn't eating—he knew. He knew everything Kiren was thinking.

"Are you getting some help? Do you have someone you can talk to?"

Okay, almost everything.

"Like who?" He had left one hospital to work pick up shifts, he was the new guy, the one that was on for one shift here, another shift there. Maybe at practicals, if he wasn't too tired to make friends.

He didn't have time to talk. Hell, if he didn't get to work Christmas Eve, he'd be fired.

One more semester.

That was all he needed.

One more and the urgent care office downtown wanted him there, eight to five.

Kiren leveled him with a look. "Like a therapist, Flynn."

"No. I'm taking the kids to their appointments, like clockwork."

Kiren's brow furrowed, frown lines deep and angry, and he stared at hard at Flynn. Then he shoved back from the table, took his plate to the sink and braced his hands on the counter. "What is your point, Flynn?"

"Uh…that the kids are going to the therapist like we agreed?" He had no idea what he'd done. None.

But that was it, wasn't it?

He was always in trouble and exhausted, and he was finished.

Kiren turned around, looking pale, and sighed. "All I've heard since I got here is how tired you are, how much you have done, how busy you've been, all the things you do for the kids—as if I do absolutely nothing. As if you're the only one, Flynn. As if I don't make all the same sacrifices. You don't make any room for the idea that maybe I'm just as fucking tired as you are."

"I wasn't talking about you. I assume you take the kids to the fucking therapist on your days. I didn't say a single fucking thing about you. No one said you didn't do anything!"

Kiren shook his head. "Okay. Fine. Just please stop shouting at me."

"Wait, so you get to accuse me of disrespecting you, but I defend myself, I'm the bad guy? How the fuck did we end up married?" Kiren didn't even *like* him.

"We were nicer to each other." Kiren dropped his gaze to the floor and turned around to pour another mug of coffee.

"No shit on that. I just wish we'd figured this shit out before we decided to involve kids." He'd honestly thought they were going to be forever.

"The kids are loved, and they're going to be fine. But I

don't have anything figured out. Not a damn thing. I just know I can't handle *this* anymore."

He got it. He didn't want to be the bad guy. He didn't want to work and study and deal and then pretend that he wasn't worn out, down to the bone. He didn't want to be a single dad. He didn't want any of this. "Well, you won't have to soon. Your mom and my dad say they'll even handle the drop-offs and pick-ups. You'll be able to move on and not deal with my shit. I hope that makes it better for you."

It wasn't going to make it easier for him.

"It won't. It's not going to. It's never going to be better. Easier maybe. Or maybe not even that because I won't have to see you all the time, but I will want to. And I won't have to talk to you much, except that I will miss you. And I guess we don't have to sit with each other at all the kids' events, but I still can't imagine not experiencing all of that—" Kiren set his coffee down and swiped at his eyes with both hands. "—all of that with you." Kiren's shoulders shook for a second before they just slumped, and he headed for the bedroom. "Excuse me."

The door closed quietly behind him.

"If you still want to be with me, why the fuck did you ask for a divorce?" he roared, then he pulled on his boots and coat. He would go sit in his truck, charge his phone, and pray that he didn't beat his brains out before he could get a plow up here.

3

It was dusk before pure hunger drove Kiren out of the bedroom. He'd waited as long as he could because he didn't know what he was going to say to Flynn. The only thing he knew was there was no hope of having a conversation if Flynn couldn't control the shouting.

The storm had ended, but there was so much snow on the ground and some of the drifts were so wild it was going to be a couple of days at least before he got out of there. He'd resigned himself to that fact, but still didn't know what all that time was going to look like.

The main part of the cabin was chilly, and he discovered that the stove had cooled down—not cold, but it definitely needed fuel—and Flynn was nowhere. Probably out in the fucking snow again like the idiot he was.

No, like the idiot he'd become. Flynn wasn't an idiot at all. He was just wired out of his mind and exhausted and looked like he hadn't eaten an actual meal in months. He was spinning on something—adrenaline, sleep deprivation, something—and he was just...reacting.

Kiren filled up the pellets and got the stove humming again, then stuck a couple of logs on the fire for light and a different kind of warmth. When he'd done all of that and Flynn still hadn't turned up, he pulled on his coat and opened the front door to see what he could see.

Flynn was in his truck, sound asleep. The silly son of a bitch had a death wish.

He needed to take care of himself so that he could make smart decisions.

"Third time is the charm, huh?" He stomped into his boots, zipped up his coat and trudged out in the knee-deep snow.

Damn. Some of the snow was hip deep.

He waded through the white stuff and pounded on the driver's side window.

Flynn was so deep asleep that he just blinked, staring at him like he was confused. "Kiren?"

"You're in your truck," he said loud enough to be heard through the window. Then he reached for the handle and opened the door. "Come inside. It's cold out." The truck wasn't too bad though. Cold, but Flynn must have had it running at some point. "Come on."

"Sorry. I dozed off."

Yes, he was aware. He didn't say it though, even if he wanted to.

"It's okay. I've got the place all warmed up. Come with me." Jesus, Flynn was out of it. He helped Flynn get moving, and made sure the truck door was closed tight. "I'm going to make some dinner."

"Damn, did I sleep all afternoon? Sorry, babe. I had one hell of a migraine. I hate these headaches."

"You get headaches? Since when?" Flynn never told him

about headaches. "I'm going to have to put the chain on the door to keep you from wandering outside like Jasper used to do." Sleeping all afternoon was probably a fraction of what Flynn needed.

"Oh, man. That scared the living daylights out of me. At least Cass stays put, mostly." That warm laugh made his balls ache a little bit.

That laugh was one of the many reasons why they 'ended up married' as Flynn said.

"Mostly." Jasper was a bulldozer. Cass was more of an observer. "Me too. And you ran out and bought the chain-lock that very afternoon, remember?" He remembered it well. They'd sat around the fire that night drinking and talking about what shit parents they were and how they couldn't believe anyone had trusted them with a baby.

"I do. I cussed all the way down the mountain, and I brought us burgers and beer..." Flynn shook his head. "Best burger ever."

"Oh, that was an orgasmic cheeseburger. Or maybe I'm confusing events. There was beer." He chuckled and made sure all of their snowy clothing got hung up and their boots were in the tray by the door.

"There was. It was an awful day, but good, because Jas was locked in and safe..." Flynn's expression was distant.

"He was our first. What did we know? I mean, he only made it to the driveway; it's not like he was lost for hours in the woods." Flynn might not have survived that kind of scare. Safety was important to him. Having everyone under one roof was important to him too.

Kiren rubbed his forehead. *Well, fuck.*

"Uh...what do you need? Water? Coffee? Did you take anything for the headache?" Okay, he was frustrated and angry, but he still loved Flynn. He could be a decent human at least.

"About a handful of Excedrin Migraine. I think it's the storm? Maybe stress? Maybe meanness. I'll grab us both a bottle of water, huh?"

Okay, that was calm.

"Yeah. Thanks." The storm, or the volume level. Jesus. At least Flynn wasn't shouting now. "I'll take stress for five hundred, Alex."

"The jerking motion at the corner of your eyes, or a small mint." Flynn actually chuckled.

He took his bottle of water. "What is a tic-tac!"

"Five hundred dollars to you, and that puts you in the lead." Flynn offered him a wink.

"Well, that's no surprise." He winked back. God, he didn't know what this weird little bit of normalcy was about, but he was holding onto it with both hands. "And it lasts just long enough for you to score a Daily Double on some random medical procedure from the nineteen fifties."

"Only if it's not literature. You've read everything." Flynn leaned against the counter. "Like every book on earth. Even the bad ones."

"I've read the bad ones twice." He chuckled and took a big sip of his water, then breathed out some of the tension in his shoulders. "Seriously. Stop going outside in the cold. You're freaking me out."

"I was losing my shit and making you cry. I needed to scream somewhere so you felt safe."

And as random as that may have sounded to someone else, he totally got it. "Yeah. okay. But for the record, you were losing your shit for sure, but I made myself cry."

"I still felt bad. I never wanted to be the one that hurt you." Flynn sighed softly. "I wanted to be the good guy."

"I hear you. I definitely did not want to be the asshole."

"Yeah." Flynn closed his eyes and took a deep breath. "I hate this."

"Fuck yes. I hate all of it. I hate how I am right now too." He'd never given up on anything the way he'd thrown his hands up over his marriage, and it had never once felt like the right answer. He just couldn't see a better one.

"We can't just keep beating on each other. We need to breathe. It's going to be at least two days here. If we're lucky, we're down the mountain for Christmas Eve..."

He was going to go down the mountain on a sled if he had to. No way was he missing Christmas Eve with the kids. Okay. He'd had enough therapy to figure this out. "I need you to stop shouting. What do you need from me?"

Flynn's lips twisted, and his ex's cheeks went a deep, dark red.

He smacked Flynn in the shoulder. "Jesus Christ, Flynn. I'm serious!" He was having trouble hiding his grin though.

And that blush still did it for him. So fucking pretty.

"I know! I know! I didn't say it. I didn't." Flynn's cheeks were going to melt the snow.

He gave Flynn a sidelong, teasing glance. "You know that would just make you shout too."

"I might just die of pure shock. I think I may be a virgin again." Okay, there was his cowboy. He was coming back.

"Please. We paid it forward. We're good for decades." He snorted, then laughed at his own joke like a dork. "Decades."

"Nonsense. I am totally virginal. Ask me. I'll tell you. I'm all shriveled down there." Flynn winked at him.

"Well, shit. Good thing I asked for a divorce." That was funny for all of three seconds. He caught Flynn's gaze to apologize. "Sorry. I didn't mean—that wasn't—Ugh. I'm sorry."

Flynn's lips twitched, and the motion finally resolved itself into a smile. "No. No, I hear you. We're going to have to learn to laugh about it, right? Neither one of us is going to give up the kids and walk away. You have fourteen more years of me."

"I wanted a lifetime with you." That just popped out unfiltered, and he panicked for a second but then decided he wasn't sorry he'd said it. It was the truth, and if nothing else, they needed to stay honest with each other if they planned to co-parent. They had to figure out how to communicate.

"So did I." Flynn's eyes filled with tears, and he turned away, into the kitchen. "What were you hungry for? There's soup, mac and cheese in a box..."

He watched Flynn go. Fuck him, those tears were so much harder take than the yelling. The shouting made him angry. The tears hurt. Deep. "Flynn." He took a few steps and reached out to rest a hand on Flynn's back, but pulled it back last minute.

He couldn't do that. That wasn't fair to Flynn. If he was going to do that, he needed to know—he needed to be very, very sure or he'd make this all even worse for them both.

It didn't stop his fingers from itching to touch though, to comfort, to hold his husband.

"I'm sorry. I'm trying to keep it together, babe. I promise." Flynn shook his head. "I just can't yet."

"You're exhausted, you're not eating. You don't have any way to cope; I can see that." And the more Flynn tried to keep it together, the more Kiren felt like he was falling apart.

"I—" Flynn sighed, then turned to him. "Who the fuck do I talk to when my best friend wants a divorce?"

"Am I really still your best friend?" He didn't feel like it. He felt like the enemy.

"You'll always be my best friend, even if you never speak to me again."

He didn't know what to say. He stared at Flynn, mapping the lines in Flynn's forehead and the bags under those dark, dark green eyes. "I can't even imagine never—I can't imagine." Alone at home he could justify it with a handful of reasons, and everything was clear. But here? Flynn had kissed him for the first time here. Right here in this kitchen, almost exactly where they were standing right now. It was kiss he had never forgotten, never would forget. It was the night he fell in love.

"No. I can't either." Flynn leaned forward as if to kiss him, then Kiren saw Flynn glance toward the table where the divorce papers sat, and he saw the life disappear from his husband's expression, leaving Flynn seeming a hundred years old. "But I don't have to. We're living it."

He couldn't watch what this divorce was doing to Flynn anymore. He'd never forgive himself for just letting it happen. There had to be another way. He marched over to the table, picked up the papers and threw them in the fireplace. "Now we're not."

"Kiren?" Flynn stared at Kiren, the fireplace, then his knees just gave out under him, and he landed on the floor.

"Oh, fuck." He ran to Flynn and sat on the floor with him, taking one hand and holding it between both of his. "Baby? Are you okay?"

"No. Yes. I don't… Tell me I didn't imagine that? That I'm not frozen to death in the truck."

"You're not frozen. I'm just out of my mind. I don't know what the answer is, but if it's this hard for both of us then those papers aren't it. The last day has been harder than all of the time we were living together and unhappy."

"I'm so tired—" Kiren almost growled, but then Flynn continued. "—of pretending I don't love you anymore."

He shifted to lean against the kitchen cabinets, pulled Flynn into his arms and whispered. "You weren't doing a very good job of it anyway."

"Shut up, you shit." Flynn cracked up, holding onto him, the laughter turning into soft, hitching sobs.

"I love you too." He held Flynn and let him cry, Flynn needed to release all of the crap that was eating him up. "I don't love what's happened to us; I don't love the things that finally made me suggest a divorce and—and whatever made you agree."

"No one wants to make someone stay if they're miserable. My feelings were hurt, man. I felt like I was a fuck up, like you were disappointed in me, and I'd worked so hard."

He sighed. There was so much to say about all of that, and so much to listen to also. He had reason to be miserable. Flynn had reason to have hurt feelings. It was all true at the same time, and how did they fix that? "You do work really hard."

"So do you."

The words surprised him—not because he didn't know he worked hard, but because Flynn said them.

"Thank you." He hugged Flynn a little tighter and wondered if this might be possible. If they could take all the pieces apart and put them all back together in a way that they fit better. The way they should be. "You know what I think? I think we should eat, and then we should get some sleep. Tomorrow we can talk and shovel off the deck, and make a snowman, and talk, and clean off our cars, and talk some more."

Keep their hands and their minds busy. Work some shit out.

"Okay. There's bacon for sandwiches, or we have potatoes or soup or pasta. You can pick."

"Soup. Easy and warm." Maybe he'd have a beer. "Do you want to go sit? I can handle it." He didn't know if he felt better, but he felt lighter. And he dared to be a little hopeful. That was something.

"I'll toast some bread on the fireplace to go with, fair?" Flynn stroked his cheek, the touch featherlight, sweet.

"Yeah, that would be good." It was all he could do not to kiss those fingers.

"It will." Flynn rolled his eyes. "If I don't charcoal them. Again."

"I have faith." He gave Flynn a smile. They deserved a little smile. "I don't really know why, because it's rare that I don't eat black toast up here, but I do anyway."

"Yeah. I'll pay super-duper attention, to quote Jas."

"Or, 'maybe Dad-Mom should make the toast next time.'" Jasper had started calling him Dad-Mom when he was about four. He figured it was Jas's four-year-old way of fitting their family into the common narrative. Or maybe Jas wanted a mom. Or maybe it was just because he usually made the PB and Js before school. Who knew? He figured it was accurate in any case. "That serious look on his face. Wow."

"I know. I know. Dad-Mom is the most bestest cook forever." Damn, Flynn did a wicked Jasper impersonation.

He laughed. "I am that. *Forever*." He shifted over and stood, offering Flynn a hand up. "You think you can manage it?"

"If not, it won't be the first bread I've burned, right?" Flynn winked at him and headed for the bread. "I wasn't planning on being here for too terrible long."

"I meant standing, since you collapsed like a newborn fawn, butthead, but you seem to have your legs under you now." Flynn was going to burn the bread. It was fact.

And he didn't care one bit.

4

Flynn still wasn't sure he wasn't dead.

The only reason that wouldn't be okay right now was because he wanted to see his babies again.

He wanted to listen to Jasper talk, to help Cass remember her dance routine, to lean together and snuggle.

They were beautiful and smart and theirs.

And it was fixin' to be Christmas.

Those divorce papers were still not on the table, though.

He stood there, staring into the fire, Kiren napping on the sofa after their supper.

Kiren had asked him to stop yelling, which he figured he could do now that he didn't feel like he had to shout the get Kiren to hear him. But Kiren had also asked him what he needed, and aside from the very obvious, he hadn't answered that one yet.

He needed to feel...important. Like all this bullshit he was doing was important to someone, because he wasn't doing it for fun.

Kiren had tossed those awful papers in the fire, so

maybe he was that important at least. And he was pretty sure it was more than Kiren just wanting to get laid.

Was it awful that he couldn't remember the last time they'd been intimate?

Hell, the last time they'd fucked? Jacked off. Snuggled hard?

Something?

"I miss you," he whispered. "I miss us, I miss the kids, being a family, but more than anything, I miss being yours."

"I'm awake," Kiren whispered back, eyes opening. "Come here."

He was so tired of crying.

Flynn went. There was no other choice and nothing else he'd rather do.

Kiren made room for him to stretch out like they'd done a million times to watch the fire burn and—do other things. It was a bit of squeeze, but he pressed in close, and Kiren's arm wrapped over his chest to hold him. "I miss it all too. So, whatever we didn't take the time to fix the last time, we're going to make the time to fix this time."

"Do you know how?" Because he didn't. Or if he did, he was too tired to reckon it. "I don't want a divorce. I don't want to lose you."

"I don't know how, yet. But I really can't imagine a future without you either, so we're going find a way. We just have to do it like we've done everything else good in our lives. Together."

He snuggled in. Yeah, he was totally dead, but it was okay with him. "I didn't burn the toast." Much.

Kiren chuckled in his ear. "It was definitely on the lighter side of burned. I'm so proud."

"Thank you. I'm trying." And that was no lie. As soon as he recovered from finals, he'd have ideas.

"Don't try right now, just be here with me. Enjoy the fire. I want to see if we can remember who we were."

"I have marshmallows for later." He knew Kiren loved roasted marshmallows.

"It's like you knew I was coming. Hey! We won't have to pick marshmallow out of Cass's hair."

"Oh, that's a blessing. I tell you, that's sort of hell on earth, listening to her scream." Their girl was tender headed, and those dark curls tangled so easy.

"It's a nightmare. But I can't say no to Jas when he asks, you know? And if I tell him we didn't bring any he knows I'm lying." He could feel Kiren shaking his head.

"Well, she'll be old enough to handle in by the time we come back up in the spring."

Kiren's words rang inside him.

"We."

"Yeah, I hope so—oh. Oh cool, I get to have spring break too." Kiren snorted.

"You do. My schedule is a little weird next semester." He would be doing a lot of practicals.

"Do your breaks line up? Do you know yet? I hope they do." Kiren's always did, they were in the same school system.

"I'm done with classes. I just have to pass the practicals. So I'll be in hospitals and offices and clinics a lot."

"Weird hours?" Kiren smoothed his T-shirt out across his belly.

"No. I'll be shadowing clinics and doing a few urgent care clinics. So I'll be more settled, depending on how many hospital shifts I need for money." He was looking forward to it, actually.

"Oh, that will be nice. We might get to have dinner together sometimes."

"Yeah. That's what this whole thing is for. Regular clinic

hours. Home for suppers. Home for ball games and dance. Weekends." More stability.

"I love it. I mean I knew that was in the works, but I guess I didn't realize it was so soon." Kiren sighed. "I should have asked more questions, huh?"

"I should have stopped being so goddamn angry." He'd felt used. Like Kiren didn't like him anymore.

"I still don't know why you were angry; you never actually told me. You just did a lot of shouting. A lot." Kiren's breath rustled his hair.

He didn't know what to say, exactly. "I felt like the only thing I was good for was what money I could bring in."

He felt Kiren's body stiffen up, but it was gone in a second. "That's my fault." Kiren shifted, letting him roll onto his back, and moved over him. "That is my fault. I stressed about money, but that never changed how I feel about you." Kiren stared into his eyes, and even though he hadn't seen it in a long time, he recognized the look. It was unmistakable. "I just need to kiss you to prove it."

"I think I remember how." If not, Kiren would show him. He had no doubt.

"You don't forget this kind of thing." Kiren smiled and kissed him gently, slowly. It wasn't tentative, but it was sweet, not rushed, not too heated.

Flynn hadn't forgotten. He felt as if he was a little tipsy, like the ground underneath him had dissolved. It was a long kiss, long enough that they just stared into each other's eyes for a bit after it ended.

"I love you. I never stopped loving you, even when I didn't like you all that much." Kiren winked at him. "We need to be a team again."

"I love you." It was hard to get out, so he said it again. "I love you. So much."

Kiren's eyes were full of tears, and he spoke fast, like he was afraid he wouldn't be able to get it all out. "I know. We'll figure this out. I won't do this to you again. I promise."

"I'll do… I'll do better. I'm going to get my shit together." He could, right? He could do that. He was almost done with his degree, and he was done with classes.

"I'll help. It's a lot, trying to work and go to school. I can see what it's done to you. You're so thin. You look so tired. I'm worried about you."

"I'm okay. I'm just—" He was tired. He was exhausted. "I keep crying. That's not me, babe."

"No. It's not at all. You need a lot of sleep is what you need. And to hug the kids. And a big steak." Kiren kissed his forehead.

It wasn't that, and he needed Kiren to know it. "I need you. You're my…you're my person, dammit. You're my world."

Kiren swallowed hard. "I'm yours, and you're mine. That's what we said, right? That's what we promised? I'll do better. I need you too."

"That's what we promised. That we'd stick this shit out—for better or worse." He wanted another of those kisses, and he brought their mouths together again.

"We forgot about the or worse part." Kiren returned his kiss, hungry lips hot as fire. "I need you."

"Here? Now? Or in the bed?" He was easy. This was before the fire, and it was immediate. They'd have to get the fire banked and all if they went to bed, but they'd have room to set up.

"Start here, finish there?" Kiren started unbuttoning the flannel PJ top that he'd been wearing all day. "I know, the fire. Maybe we can make out until it dies a little. We have all night."

"We do. It's cozy out here anyway." He reached up and stroked Kiren's throat. "So pretty."

"You're the only person who has ever told me that. I think it's the freckles."

"It's the whole package. You're perfect for me." He nibbled a line along Kiren's throat.

He knew how much Kiren liked that. Kiren stretched his neck, giving Flynn more room to nibble. "I'm relieved that you can still say that after everything we've been through."

Hell yes. They'd put each other through a lot.

"Love isn't our issue."

"Obviously not. Sex probably isn't either but I'm looking forward to making sure you know how much I appreciate you." Kiren's fingers worked their way under his shirt.

"I haven't… I haven't felt like even jacking off, hardly," he admitted.

"You didn't have any problem *responding* when I asked you what you needed from me." Kiren ghosted a thumb over his nipple.

"Shut up, you." He didn't ever have any problem responding to Kiren.

"Mm. Okay." He thought Kiren's tone was suggestive, and he was right. Kiren drew a wet tongue along the length of his ear and blew across it, making him shiver.

His toes curled and he couldn't fight his gasp. Oh, he felt that all the way to his balls.

"Good?" Kiren whispered in his ear, then nipped at his earlobe. "Remember our first night here?"

"How could I forget?" They'd made love for hours—tearing each other up. He'd been sore for days.

"We have that kind of time for the first time since the kids were born."

"We do. I want it. You. Us. Now. Now is good for me. And also later." He was an idiot, but he was trying.

Kiren chuckled softly. The puffs of air on his neck were followed by kisses across his throat. "You're such a dork, and I love you."

"Good. I'm..." He swallowed, Kiren hitting every hot spot he had, one by one.

"Hot? Yes, you are." Kiren's hand was roaming over his chest and shoulders, exploring underneath his shirt.

He stroked his fingers through Kiren's hair, holding him close, petting him. He was burning up.

Kiren undressed him slowly and kept him buzzing, touching and kissing anywhere and everywhere but his aching cock until the fire turned to embers and they were both breathless.

"I—Fuck, I love you." His voice was totally blown. Completely raw.

"Bed, baby?" Kiren got to his feet and looked down at him, a dark silhouette against what little was left of the firelight.

"Yeah. We can keep each other warm." He'd missed snuggling with Kiran for so long.

"Come on. I'll remind you how much I want you." Kiren offered him a hand up and led him to the bedroom.

"I like your plan." They bundled up under the blankets, the residual heat keeping the room bearable.

"Mm. This is better." Kiren stretched him out, lips working their way across his chest.

He reached down, searching out his lover in the dark, relearning the beloved body by touch. Kiren nuzzled his belly, moving lower, one hand sliding down his thigh.

He stared up into the darkness of the blanket, and he spread, letting Kiren in to touch him.

"You're going to feel so good. I'm going to send you into outer space." He felt the breath on his balls first, then Kiren's hot tongue, teasing and tasting him.

"Don't want to be in outer space. Want to be right here with you. Right fucking here."

Kiren's fingers curled around his shaft, and he hummed and lapped at Flynn's balls.

Flynn reckoned he would just die—just expire of sheer joy right here.

"I got you. Wherever you go, I'll be right there." That wet tongue slid higher, drawing a line up his length before slowly bathing the head of his cock.

"Wherever... Turn around. I want you too. Please." He wanted to taste his lover as well.

"Fuck, yeah." Kiren tugged at the blankets to make some headroom and turned around, straddling him. The heavy cock hit him in the chin, and Kiren groaned.

"That's it." He whimpered, opening up to slap the sweet prick with his tongue. It was easier to be confident like this, in the dark.

Kiren didn't hesitate another second and took his cock in deep, swallowing around the head.

His entire soul hiccupped, and he grabbed Kiren's hips, dragging that sweet cock into his throat.

Kiren let him go long enough to gasp and curse, and then went right back to his cock, stroking as that tongue drove through his slit. It was maddening, absolutely driving him out of his mind, and all Flynn could do was give as good as he got.

But Kiren didn't make it easy. After another breath, Kiren worked hard, taking him in deep and making it tough to concentrate.

Kiren was wild enough that Flynn was dizzy, but who cared? He was lying down and holding on tight.

Kiren's cock was hard as diamonds and leaking, the bitter and salty taste covering his tongue. He closed his eyes and sucked, tongue slapping the heavy veins along the shaft, driving him mad.

"I want to fuck your mouth," Kiren whispered roughly.

His answer was to grab Kiren's ass and pull hard, making his offer clear.

"Fuck!" Kiren's cry was muffled by the comforter but seemed loud all the same. Those hips started to move, rocking and shoving that cock into his mouth.

He opened, letting Kiren in deep, swallowing hard every time the tip of his cock slipped into his throat.

Kiren shivered and moaned, letting his cock go to suck in a breath. "Flynn. Close, baby."

Come for me. Come on. I need you. I need to feel you. Taste you.

The grunt was familiar and the long moan too. Kiren came in strong waves, giving him everything he wanted.

Almost everything.

Kiren didn't wait to catch his breath before diving back to work, sucking and stroking him, turning his sweet ache into something more.

"Love. Love. Fuck, I need you..." He was babbling. He knew it.

Kiren answered by rolling his balls in hot fingers and humming around the head of his cock.

He didn't have another second to hold on, and he didn't even try. He shot hard enough his bones rattled, and his eyes rolled up into his head.

When he came back down a bit, Kiren turned back around, settling in beside him. Kiren tugged the covers down a little and they both breathed in the fresh air, which didn't seem that chilly yet, but would soon enough.

"Love you." He did, and he wanted to chat, but he was so fucking sleepy, and Kiren was right there, holding him.

"Mhm. Love you. I've got you." Kiren pressed a kiss to his temple. "Sleep, baby. All you want. It's just you, me, and the snow."

"You. Me." He liked that. He liked that in his bones.

5

Flynn owed him one.

When Kiren got out of bed the cabin was freezing. He added pellets to the stove and lit a few logs in the fireplace. Flynn hadn't even stirred when he started a fire in the little pot belly stove in the bedroom.

He'd had breakfast and lunch; the cabin was toasty now and, although he'd been up for hours, he was glad that Flynn was sleeping in. Flynn could sleep all day for all he cared; his husband obviously needed the rest.

They had power back since it had stopped snowing, and the solar panels were doing their jobs, so now it was just a matter of waiting for the plow. That could take a day or two, but he was okay with that. They had good news for the kids when they could get out, and until then, Flynn could rest, and Kiren would feed him until he popped.

"Mmm...you started the fire." Flynn wandered out, looking like a mummy. "What time is it?"

"Um..." He looked at his watch. "About four." He got up, setting the book he was reading down on the coffee table. "Cold?"

"I guess?" Flynn came right to him, searching his eyes. "I didn't dream it, right?"

He shook his head and smiled. "No, you didn't dream that. Hopefully you dreamed lots of other good things. You slept right through lunch."

"I only eat once a day if that, but I hate that I missed the time with you. I need to get us home for Christmas Eve. I need our babies to be with us."

"If that? Since when? No wonder your jeans are falling right off you. I'll make you a dinner you can't refuse." They would see the kids soon, but barring a miracle, it wasn't going to be today.

"I just...haven't been hungry."

Which was why he'd wanted Flynn to see a therapist, dammit.

"Yeah, well, you burned up some calories last night." He steered Flynn over to the couch to sit. "The snow stopped this morning, but the radio says the road is still not passable. Maybe tomorrow." Hopefully tomorrow. He didn't want to miss Christmas.

"I'll get us down, if we have to snowshoe to the road and snowmobile the rest of the way..."

"We can't snowmobile all the way home, baby, we need at least one car. Relax. We'll get there." Until then, they had uninterrupted time to snuggle and deal with their shit. He didn't see a downside.

"Right." Flynn reached for him, holding him close. "I just don't want to disappoint you or the kids."

"The kids are little. If we miss the actual day, I'll tell Mom to say the next day is Christmas. They won't even know." He kind of liked the idea that any day could be Christmas.

Flynn chuckled softly. "Ho ho ho, Santa Daddy?"

He snorted. "How did you manage to make that sound so dirty?"

Flynn chuckled, the sound low and husky. "I'm pure sex, doncha know?"

"Oh, I know." He nuzzled Flynn's neck, inhaling the scent of man and lovemaking. "I very much know. I'd forgotten for a minute, but I won't again."

"Oh." That earned him a surprised blink that melted into a warm, pleased little grin.

"So I've been thinking while you were sleeping." He pulled Flynn to the couch in front of the fire. "Do you have more time off after Christmas? Or are you going right back to work?"

"Shit, I'm lucky if I have a job after this. I'll just have to take shifts, but this next semester?" Flynn shrugged and offered him a little grin. "I'm working for free, for the most part, but I have a job offer starting as soon as I pass my boards. Eight to five, Monday through Friday."

"Okay, well that's good in a way. I was thinking that we should sit down after Christmas and work on our schedules so we're on the same page. You know, family calendar and all that. If it's about taking shifts at the hospital, then we'll figure out the couple of times that you really need to be home so you'll know when it's all good." They got off track because they were so busy they didn't communicate, and Flynn was killing himself over it. He didn't want that to happen again.

"It should be easier, right? When we're both on the same basic schedule?"

Kiren nodded, then tilted his head. "Where are you going to work?"

"I got offered a position at a general practice—mostly the day-to-day stuff, but I will get to know my patients, and

I'll have the opportunity to come home. I can even do video visits from home."

Wow. That sounded...great, actually. "Hey, that sounds like a good opportunity. So you took it?"

"Yeah. I mean, I have to finish this semester, pass my tests, but...yeah." Flynn shrugged and smiled. "It's why I went back to school, right?"

"It is. And you're smiling about it now, so I like that better." He kissed Flynn's cheek. His husband was so handsome when he smiled.

"It was killing me. So much money and time, and I was scared I was going to fail..." Why hadn't Flynn told him?

"I wish I'd known." That sounded better than 'why did you say something' right? Maybe? "I could have helped."

"I was ashamed, and then it was too late..."

What? "Too late? When did it become too late?"

"Well, once we started fighting, I guess?"

He sighed. "I'm not ashamed of you. I have never been. You shouldn't be ashamed to be honest with me. Okay? Please?"

"You know that I'm not the best at school. I have to try a little harder than some of these folks, but I'm doing it. I did it. I did the schooling part. I'm going to ace the practicals." Flynn squeezed his hand, holding on tight.

Kiran squeezed back. He wanted Flynn to understand. "I'm proud of you. I knew you could do it. I didn't know it was so frustrating for you, though."

"I was losing my mind. I swear to God, between the kids, school, the hospital, and our fights—I wanted to give up a few times."

"When I showed up before the storm, you looked like you had." He'd never seen anyone looking so thin and exhausted. "You've made yourself sick."

"Yeah."

No argument. No bullshit.

Just 'yeah'.

He nodded and pulled Flynn closer. "Yeah." What else was there to say? "I'm not going to let you do this again."

"Okay. I can live with that. I just want to be able to spend time with all y'all."

"We'll just start over, that's all. We'll rebuild it, you know? Just...begin again. Fresh. New." But with kids and a house.

"I can come home?"

Oh, God. How was that not clear to Flynn already? "Baby. Yes. God, yes."

"Thank you." Flynn let out a huge breath, his eyes closing. "I'm coming home."

"You are home. This is home too. We have so many good memories here, don't we?" He shifted and slid off the couch. "You know what you need? Food. Tell me what you're craving." He had one more day to feed his husband before they could head back to the kids, and he was going to use it well.

"Honestly? I would give about anything for your spaghetti. I dream about it, sometimes."

"I can totally do that." Maybe he could do a fakey garlic bread with some toast. "You should not need to be dreaming about food. Was money really that bad?"

"No. Yes. Sometimes I fed the kids and ate at the hospital."

Shit. He'd been fine for money, and he'd had help from his parents with the kids. Flynn probably would have gotten some alimony, but...well. He was glad they didn't have to go there anymore.

"Extra meatballs for you. Or whatever I can find."

"There are hamburger patties in the cooler outside." Flynn winked at him, gaze embarrassed. "I'm going to make good money once the summer's here. I'm going to make good money, and there isn't any debt from the school, so—"

"We're okay. I can get us that far. I just want you to focus on your boards and the kids." And sleeping. And eating. And if he had to ask his parents for a little boost, he just would. They would understand, especially his mom. She adored Flynn.

They'd be okay.

"Are you dressed under there? Grab the beef for me?"

"Mmhmm." Flynn winked at him. "I guess I can do that. You want another beer? There are four left."

"Yes, please. Definitely. It's not like we're driving anywhere." Which reminded him, he needed to call Mom.

He started the water boiling and got out some seasonings for the meatballs, then dialed Mom, putting the phone on speaker.

"Oh, thank goodness, Kiren. I was getting worried. Are you almost here?"

He rolled his eyes. "No, Mom. We're still snowed in. I think we'll be able to get out tomorrow."

"Son! Should I call the state police? Are you all right? Is Flynn?"

"We're fine, Mom. We have lots of food and wood. We're good. And I mean...*we're* good too. Flynn and I. You'll see us both tomorrow."

"What?" That was pure shock, and it made him chuckle. "Both? You mean...are you saying you'll both be here to pick up the children?"

"I am. We'll both be there tomorrow, and we'll both be going back to the house." He glanced up to find Flynn listening in. "Flynn is right here. Say hi, Mom."

"Hi, Mom."

"Flynn? Honey? Are you well? Are you ready for Christmas?"

"No? Yes? I just want to come home."

"I'm so glad we'll be seeing you. I hope Kiren is taking good care of you."

"Mom!"

"What? I want you both happy and whole. Do you want to talk to the kids?"

"Yes," he and Flynn said at the same time. He took the hamburger from Flynn and winked at him.

"Say hi to your daddies."

"Hi, Daddy! Hi, Dad-Mom!"

"Hey, guys!"

"Are you snow—snow—snow-ded?"

"Snowed in," Mom corrected gently.

"We are, but we're together and safe. We miss y'all like crazy!" Flynn lit up. "Cr-aaaa-zy!"

"Cr-aaaa-zy!" The kids echoed. Kiren loved the way it made Flynn's smile even brighter.

"Are you being good for Gramma?"

"Jas had to sit on the stairs."

"Cas won't take a bath!"

Mom sighed. "We're fine. Don't you two worry about anything. Just get back here safely tomorrow. Promise?"

"I'll get him home. I swear, Mom. I'll get him home." Flynn chuckled. "You hooligans be good for Granny, do you hear me?"

Cas quickly said, "Yes, Daddy!" The raspberry in the background sounded like Jas.

"Jas, you need to take care of Gramma for me. Be a big boy okay?"

"Okay, Dad-Mom."

"Okay. Good." Mom chuckled. "I think I better make dinner; they're getting hangry. We'll see you tomorrow. Night, boys."

Mom hung up, and he put his phone down.

"Those two." He shook his head and got to work making meatballs.

"They're amazing. What did you get them from Santa?" Flynn sat on one of the little rickety chairs.

"I got them bikes. Jas's is a crazy bright green, and Cas's is one of those balance ones that doesn't have pedals. It's cute." Jas had been begging for a bike. "How about you?"

Flynn rolled his eyes. "I got them bikes. One green and one purple."

Of course. Because they listened to their kids, and that's what they would have done if they'd been together. "Yep. Purple. It's her favorite color." He grinned and Flynn grinned back, and then they were cracking up, laughing together like that hadn't in over a year.

He shook his head, still chuckling. "I'll return mine. We need more presents. We better stop on the way home tomorrow."

"Are yours put together? Because mine aren't. I was going to do it Christmas Eve..."

"Oh. No. Actually, I was going to do it yesterday, but—" He laughed again. "Nope. I guess we have some work to do tomorrow night."

"It'll go faster together. We can share a bottle of wine and play with tools."

"I'm not sure it will go faster with wine, but it will be more fun at least." He put the meatballs in a pan, and they started sizzling. "We are ridiculous, huh?"

"I think you're amazing. I want you to believe that I am too. I need that."

"I meant all the fighting; that was ridiculous. I do think you're amazing, and I tried to prove it to you last night. We just have to—talk. Talk more. Be honest. Ask for help. Say our feelings are hurt. Whatever, you know? So we don't end up here again."

Flynn nodded to him. "I think you're right. I think we have to be...vulnerable to one another. Open."

Open. Yeah, that was the right word. And he needed to take better care of Flynn. He wasn't going to say that out loud, but he knew. He'd known it when they were married, but with the kids and money and time...he'd forgotten. He'd forgotten how happy it made him when Flynn was happy.

"I can do that. Can you?"

"Yes. And if I don't, ask me. I want us. I need us."

He stepped around the kitchen island and pulled Flynn into a hug. "I love you. I'm not going to let this happen to us again."

"Okay. I believe you." Flynn held on tight, lips on his jaw. "I believe in us."

He took a kiss that went on longer than he'd intended and pulled away with a smile. "Pasta. And then we should get on the radio and see when they plan to get us out tomorrow."

Not if. When.

"Right. There are bicycles to build, and babies to kiss on."

"How long do cowboys call their kids babies?" He teased as he stirred the meatballs around and put the spaghetti in the boiling water.

"Until the cowboys are in the grave." There wasn't a hint of hesitation.

He rolled his eyes. "So dramatic."

"Yep, but it's true. My momma still calls me her baby."

Flynn grinned at him, winked. "And I'm getting up there in years."

"Oh, yeah. You're a whole month older than I am. You're ancient. A fossil." Flynn loved to say he was old. Or maybe he just loved to hear Kiren tell him he wasn't.

"Oooh. A fossil. Is that why I'm so hard?" Flynn waggled his eyebrows.

"No, that's just your natural state when you're around me because I am so sexy." Kiran waggled his eyebrows and posed stupidly, making himself laugh.

"You so are." It was amazing, to be watched like Flynn saw him.

"Okay. Set the table, find some candles, and we'll do this up right."

"Yeah, the solar lights aren't going to hold up long, are they? We'll be romantic." Flynn dug out a set of candles, lit them, and put dishes on the table. "I'll pull in a bucket of snow to melt for dishes after too."

"Sounds good. The power's been on and off if you want to charge your phone."

"I'll charge it in the truck tomorrow. It's dead-dead, but the sat phone's good."

"Cool. My cell's working obviously, we had power when I woke up."

"Yeah, we got enough sun to charge us for a bit." Flynn was so much more at home up here in the cabin than Kiren was. He'd spent every summer up here until he was grown. Then he'd been with the rodeo, traveling and doing sports medicine.

"Does it ever bother you, that you're not traveling all the time? That you have a house, a job, a family?"

Flynn shot him a look. "Lots of rodeo jobs have a home,

a day job, family, you know. And no, I did all this work to be with you guys *more*."

"I just know you loved it. You probably miss all the action." Flynn had started changing his whole life after they'd decided to get married. It was a lot to ask of someone.

"I missed being a part of something. I hated being always on the bottom rung of the ladder at the hospital. It was demoralizing as fuck."

"I'm sorry. I wish you'd told me more, but I get it, I guess. We want to feel like we can handle things. Sometimes we can't, you know?"

"Sometimes we can't." Flynn met his eyes. "I was so jealous of you. It felt like you were so together, and I just kept fucking up."

"Looking like I have it together is my superpower." Sometimes he did, but mostly he put on a good show. He was lucky; he had help. Flynn didn't. "You kept trying, and you did it. That's not fucking up, baby. That's winning."

"I am a good nurse. I'm really good. My patients are going to love me."

"There you go. See? You're amazing." He'd gotten lucky in a way, deciding he wanted to teach. He just got a job, and he was doing it, and he loved it. The kids seemed to love him too. "It's good to have that confidence and also that validation."

"Well, part of it is hope, but the fact that I already have a position lined up is super positive."

"Hope is good. So is spaghetti and meatballs. Sit, baby, let me feed you." Kiran carried the bowls to the table and pulled out Flynn's chair.

That was what they both needed. Some comfort food, and hope.

6

The morning of Christmas Eve was bitter cold and sunny, so that was how Flynn knew it was time to get down the hill. He'd been up at five a.m., dealing with getting the state police to have CDOT come get them.

He let Kiran sleep in while he packed up the cab of the truck and started the process of closing the cabin until spring.

His world had totally changed in the last forty-eight hours.

It started with the lowest moment of his whole life—pen in hand, reading divorce papers—and now he was headed home hand in hand with his husband.

Well, truck and SUV trundling down the mountain with his husband...

"I see sunshine." Kiren came out of the bedroom fully dressed, hair neat and smiling. "Tell me we're going home."

"They're working their way up. We should be down by noon. Will that give us enough time to do Christmas shopping?"

"Sure, we can go before we go to Mom's house and wrap

stuff after they go to bed." Kiren rolled his eyes. "While we're building bikes. I bet Dad will help. What can I do around here? You're closing up?"

"I don't imagine we'll be back for the rest of the winter, eh? We can plan a long visit together when you're on break, maybe." They could make a plan in May, after his test and graduation.

"Yeah, probably not. Spring break maybe. We'll see. Maybe we'll try to go somewhere warm if you can get the time off."

"Well, there will be a week or two between. Maybe we can go on a cruise..."

"Huh. That's a great idea. Let's look into it." Kiren started poking around helping with the little things he always did to close up the house. "Is the cooler in your truck yet?"

"Yeah. I left the milk out in the snow for you."

"Ooh. Thank you so much." Kiren opened the back door and grabbed it. "Brrr. Do you need coffee?"

He could feel it, the way things were starting to normalize between them. Kiren was just—doing what he always did, no tension, no worry.

"I think I will, yeah. I'm going to bring a new French press up next time."

"That's a good idea. This one has definitely seen better days." Kiren got the water going on the stove and pulled out two mugs.

"Yeah. I worried it was going to just go boom, but it held on."

"Well, it's got one more chance." Kiren laughed and moved back a few steps dramatically.

"Lord, you do tempt fate." Flynn grabbed Kiren, dragged him close, and kissed the fire out of him.

"Mm!" Kiren smiled against his lips and hugged him. "Someone is in a good mood."

"I'm coming home. I'm coming to sleep with you. What's not to be in a good mood for?"

"Truth, my husband. So true." Kiren kissed him back. "Honeymoon is over though. After Christmas it's back to work and school and karate and dance class and snotty little four-year-old colds."

"I deal with tons of those. I maintain our children are the worst."

"Right? They must have gotten that from you." Kiren winked and slipped away to pour their coffee.

"Oh ho! I am damn charming when I'm sick, thank you!" He goosed Kiren on the way.

"Ow!" Kiren swatted at him. "You are not charming when you're sick; you're a big baby with the man-flu." Kiren paused a second, coffee pot in hand. "Or maybe that's me."

"Actually, you're a good patient. You take your meds, follow instructions, and sleep." He hated being sick. He had too damn much to do to be down in the mouth.

"I'm so boring." Kiren handed him a mug of coffee. "Man. I am ready to get out of here. Not that I don't enjoy the cabin, but you know what I mean."

"I do. This is a fun place in the summer and fall, but it's Christmas, and it's time to be home with the beasts." He would make cinnamon toast pancakes for Christmas morning.

Kiren sipped his coffee again, and then they both heard the rumbling. "Plow!"

"Oh, thank God. Do you think you can drive down? I can try to tow you, but..." It was dangerous.

"Yeah. I can drive. You got me that giant all-wheel drive for a reason, right? I'll follow you." He heard the words, and he saw the nod, but he wasn't sure how much confidence there was behind it.

"I'll be right there. We get down the mountain and on the road, then we'll be golden." He wasn't going to let Kiren wreck.

"Yep. No problem. And then home to the kids. I can't wait." Kiren took his mug and washed both of them. "What's left? Are we ready?"

"We are. Let's get the engines warming up." He met Kiren's eyes. "It's not going to disappear when we get down the mountain, is it?"

He didn't want to have this new chance dissolve.

Kiren held his gaze, moved in close again and put an arm around him. "No. It's going to get even better."

"I believe you." And even if he didn't, Flynn would work on it until he did.

"Good. I'm ready if you're ready." Kiren let him go. "Just need my boots." They'd dug the trucks out yesterday and he'd made sure they both started up, so at least he knew they were good on that front.

"Yeah, bundle up, and we'll figure out where we're heading after we get into town."

"Maybe we can stop and grab the kids some doughnuts from that bakery. That would be a good excuse to pull over a minute after the drive down the mountain, right?" Yeah, Kiren was nervous. He heard that loud and clear.

"Hey, if the team has two people, I'll see if one can drive your SUV down and you can ride with me."

"I can do it. I want to. Man up, right? I'll just follow you. You'll get me down okay." That much Kiren sounded confident about.

"I will. I promise." He gave Kiren another kiss. "I have another chance with you. I'm not going to mess it up."

"No one's going to mess anything up. We're just starting fresh, and we'll handle things as they come up this time. Okay?" He reached out to help Kiren with his coat and Kiren let him, smiling. "Thank you. I'm ready."

"I am too. I love you." He took a deep breath and opened the door. It was time to get them down the mountain.

7

Flynn pulled off at the bottom of the access road, and Kiran followed into the little parking lot willingly. The drive down hadn't been as bad as he'd feared, but it wasn't easy either. Not for him anyway. Flynn had made it look easy, leading him around corners and keeping his speed in check, and the next thing he knew, they'd made it.

He trusted Flynn more than anyone else in his life, and Flynn earned it again and again. He wasn't sure what to think of himself now. Surely he would have changed his mind before their court date. Maybe at mediation or maybe in the middle of a lonely night. Maybe Flynn would have put up more of a fight about him, not just the kids.

Maybe. Hopefully. But it didn't matter now.

They only stopped long enough for Flynn to check on him and get a hug – so fucking sweet—and then they were on the road again.

He decided he should call Mom to let her know and give her an ETA.

"Are you okay? Is Flynn? Where are you? What do you

need from me? What can I do? Why are you two keeping that damn cabin?"

Jesus. What was up? She'd been cool as a cucumber yesterday. He decided not to answer the ridiculous questions, like why keep the cabin. She probably wouldn't understand the answers anyway. "Hi, Mom. We're fine. We just made it down the mountain, so we're maybe an hour away after we shop. I wanted to give you an ETA."

Her snort was epic. *Epic*. "Uh-huh. If you think for one second that is all you're going to say to me now that the children are with their grandfather, and I'm cooking like a fiend, you've lost your damn mind."

"Flynn and I are back together. Doesn't that make you happy? What else would you like me to say? What are you cooking? I can't wait." Surely that would distract her, right?

"I would like you to tell me what you two said to one another that ended almost a year of pain and sorrow and upheaval."

"I know, I hear you. But it's not even what was said, you know? I mean, we said some things, sure. We fought first and then we listened, but Mom, you have to see him. He's skinny and exhausted...he looks like a ghost. And he loves the kids so much."

"You can't fix him, baby. You know that. You can't make him not a workaholic or a people pleaser."

It wasn't a fixing issue. It was, well, at the end of the day it was a money issue. "He's not a workaholic. And what's wrong with wanting to make his family happy?" He didn't understand. Why couldn't Mom be as happy as he was?

"Nothing. I'm tickled to death. You know I love Flynn like he was my own—"

There was a but coming. There was always a but, with that tone.

"—But I worry that things aren't really fixed, just ignored."

"It's not that they're fixed so much as, it's...we're on the same page finally, you know? We figured it out. I know what he needs, and he knows what I need. Now we just have to be more mindful and not make the same mistakes again." That was right. Mindful. Respectful. "We need to communicate better. We know it's not perfect yet."

Flynn could do it; he knew his husband wanted this more than anything. Flynn could talk more, not hide things, right?

"I'm just scared. You've been so unhappy, and the kids are just now settling, but... God, baby, I hope you're right. I've been wishing hard for this. You two are meant to be together, but you're both so..."

He frowned. "Both so what?"

"Stubborn. You're both just bullheaded as hell."

He sighed loud enough he knew his mother heard it. "Whatever, Mom." Sure, they both could be stubborn, but who couldn't?

"It's true. And you both have to figure this out. Together. You both have to give and take."

"We're working on it. We were stuck in a cabin for two days withing nothing to do but talk, Mom." Well, talk and make love, but Mom didn't need the details.

"Uh-huh..."

"Mom!"

"What? I'm not stupid."

"Fine. But that wasn't all of it. And we *are* married, you know." Was he supposed to be listening to this? Questioning what he and Flynn had already worked out?

"I'm glad you two finally remembered that." She

chuckled softly. "And I'm making jalapeno popper dip. Flynn loves it."

His sigh was relieved this time. "He really does. Thanks, Mom, I appreciate it. And please don't worry. We're going to be okay. Better even. I promise."

"It's my job. Are you two shopping? If you are, can you pick up some pecans and some rum for me?"

"We are and we will." He knew what that meant. Pie. He loved pie. "Need anything else? We're probably going to run to Target too."

"Uh...crayons and coloring books. Pajamas that match for you two. Something for your father's stocking."

"I'm on it." He winced a little at the pajamas—of course she wouldn't have bought any since Flynn wasn't coming. They'd have fun picking them out. "Love you, Mom. See you soon."

"Be careful. Love you." She hung up and he took a deep breath. Lord, she was a firecracker, but she had his best interests at heart.

Flynn moved into the left lane, and he followed. "Good Idea, baby," he said out loud. "Let's get home already."

"Hey, Dad." Flynn had a headache that would not quit.

"Hey. What's wrong? You sound like shit. Should we drive up?" His folks were in Glenwood, and he didn't need them driving in this storm, even if it was just a couple hours.

"No. No. I—I'm getting back together with Kiren." With his husband.

The long pause before Dad answered spoke volumes. "O—kay."

"I know. He came to the cabin. He threw the divorce papers in the fire. He says he wants to try again, and I want to too. Tell me I'm not stupid."

"You're not stupid. But are you thinking clearly? A grand gesture and a lot of talk doesn't earn someone forgiveness."

"No." And he hadn't expected to get it, but—"I love him. I want my family back. I want my kids every day. I want to go home."

"You do know that I meant it doesn't earn him *your* forgiveness, right? You have been doing everything you can for those kids. You're working your ass off. Don't be a pushover, Flynn. He needs to prove he deserves for you to come back."

"I'm not a pushover. What good am I doing any of us like it is? I hate it. I want to try. We'll do therapy or whatever, but I miss my life." And he didn't want to do this anymore. He didn't want to be a single dad.

"I get it. But you're *so*—and he's *so*—" Dad sighed. "You know. But I like him. You know I do."

"I do too. I just want him to try and have my back for a few more months." He just needed Kiren to believe in him, to trust him.

"I hope he can. Your mother, and I just want you to be happy. And you know how we feel about those kids. I'm rooting for you, kid."

"Good. Just...pray for me, huh? I need all the help I can get."

"Every day. We miss you. Merry Christmas, son."

"Merry Christmas Eve, Dad. We'll call tomorrow, okay?"

"And we'll come up for New Years. It'll be fun."

He nodded as if Dad could see him. "It will. Love you, Old Man."

"Shut up, son. Be careful. Text me when you're home."

"Yes, sir." He hung up and grinned. His dad always said that, and he said it to the kids every time they left with Kiran. Maybe he wouldn't have to do it anymore.

8

It never ceased to amaze Kiren how resilient his children were. Daddy and Dad-Mom weren't happy and were living separately for a while, and now they were happy again and everything was good.

Done. Accepted. Moving on.

At least for now.

Jasper had squinted at them until they confirmed that Flynn was actually staying for dinner and would definitely make them breakfast in the morning, and then that seemed to be that.

Jasper was in the shower now, and Flynn had just finished giving Cassidy a bath. He was listening to her giggle and Flynn's deeper chuckle as he combed through the presents they'd bought on their way to his parents' house.

"Well, this certainly is nice, having everyone here again for Christmas." His mother never missed a beat. She knew he was alone so she could ask all of her questions.

"It is, right? And it will be a typically long night of wrapping."

"I still worry."

"Mom. We talked about this already."

"Yes, but what did he say to convince you?"

"He said—well, what he said isn't important. He didn't have to say anything, Mom. You saw him. And that's after me feeding him and making him sleep for three days." It was going to take a while to undo everything their separation had done to Flynn.

"Yes, but I want this to be more than you feeling sorry for him. I want you both to be happy." Mom adored Flynn, so it felt like she was looking out for both of them.

"I know. I love him. I don't feel sorry for him; I was worried about him. It's not pity; it's love. I forgot all the reasons I married him in the first place, you know? He's been reminding me." And it wasn't perfect yet; they both had work to do still. He knew that. But it felt like work worth doing now instead of something he wanted to give up on.

"Well, good then. This whole thing was stupid. You two are amazing, and giving up when things get hard is ridiculous."

He stared at his mother. "What happened to you're both so stubborn'?"

"You are." She winked at him. "But he makes you smile. He always has."

He rolled his eyes. "I suppose that's better than 'I told you so'. I tossed the paperwork in the fireplace. I just couldn't take it, seeing him hurting like that. He was desperate to see the kids, but I'm glad we had a few days to talk and just be together."

"We'd be happy to babysit once a month to give you time to reconnect."

He smiled because that offer was both selfless and selfish, and they made him equally happy. "Thank you. I think we'll take you up on that."

"Good. He's a hard worker, a good provider, a great dad, and he loves you." Mom kissed his cheek. "And so do I."

"Yeah, yeah. I need to help tuck the kids in. Do you feel like wrapping?" He grinned at her, knowing she'd say yes even if she didn't really feel like it. It was Christmas after all.

"Of course. Then I'm going to pour a glass of wine and put on *White Christmas*."

"Sounds great. Thanks, Mom." He kissed her cheek and went to find Flynn. The kids had spent so many nights here they were comfortable, and it had been a tradition for Santa to visit here instead of home, so he was glad that nothing was changing for them this year.

Flynn was rocking Cass, singing carols with her and Jasper, the low voice sweet and slow.

He sat with Jasper and joined in, putting an arm around their son. When the song ended, he squeezed Jasper's shoulders and whispered, "Bedtime, guys. Santa can't come if you're not asleep."

"You'll both be here in the morning?" Cass grinned when Flynn nodded.

"I'll be here for Santa, and then we'll have the day here before we go home tomorrow night, cool?"

"Cool." Jasper hopped up and moved over to his bed.

Kiren loved this room. It had been his as a kid, and now to have his children in it just made him happy. He tucked Jasper in, and then switched places with Flynn. "Goodnight, Cass. Sleep tight."

"Merry Christmas Eve! It's going to be the best Christmas ever!"

"That's right. The best ever." He kissed her forehead, glad to be here and not stuck in that cabin anymore. He went to Flynn and took his hand as they left the room together. "Feeling better?"

"Mmhmm. It's good to see their baby faces." Flynn squeezed his hand and leaned in, taking a quick kiss.

"I know, right? Next up bicycles. Mom is wrapping the stuff we bought for us. Should we go help her first?" They probably should, but really, he wanted a glass of wine.

"Whatever you want. Is she mad?"

"Mom?" He laughed. "No, baby. She's very happy. She apparently had more faith in us than we did."

"I do like her." Flynn bumped their shoulders together. "Almost as much as I like you."

"I'll keep her. She's a free babysitter after all." He was going to keep her offer to take the kids once a month to himself so he could surprise Flynn and take him out. Kiran thought his husband—his husband, dammit—would be thrilled with a date night.

They hadn't done that in a long time.

Maybe New Year's Eve when Flynn's parents were visiting and could watch the kids. That could be a lot of fun.

He kept hold of Flynn's hand as they went back downstairs. "You want a glass of wine while we build those bikes?"

"Oh, we are living dangerously, are we?" Flynn chuckled but nodded. "Why not? We've earned a glass."

"We've earned a whole bottle, but the bikes might not be safe to ride if we go there." He pulled Flynn into the kitchen and found an open bottle on the counter. "Dad beat us to it."

"You know he's waiting with the power tools, and Mom's got one eye on the stairs making sure Jasper doesn't cheat."

He had to grin because he was sure Flynn was right. "You know them so well." He poured two glasses and handed one to Flynn. "Let's go rescue Dad."

"Sounds great. We'll pretend we can read instructions,

he'll pretend he knows everything, and Mom will roll her eyes."

"Instructions? What are instructions?"

When they got to the garage, Dad was already there, wine on the workbench and reading glasses on his nose. Dad glanced up at them. "I think we can handle this."

"I hope so, because they're the big Santa gift." Flynn rolled his eyes, but the grin was wide and happy. "Hey, you. It's good to be here."

"Good to have you back." Dad shook Flynn's hand and covered it with his free one for a second before letting Flynn go. That was honest affection from his father, and he knew it wasn't lost on his husband.

"I say we start with the small one."

"You start with Cassidy's little one. Flynn and I will work on Jasper's." Dad handed Flynn a box cutter and that was apparently that.

He managed to meet Flynn's eyes long enough to give him a playful wink.

Flynn waggled his eyebrows, and it felt so good, to play, to be relaxed.

Relaxed for a few minutes anyway. Cassidy's bike didn't even have pedals, but it was still complicated to assemble. He did get it done though, and before Dad and Flynn had finished Jasper's.

"You men need any help?" he teased, reaching for what was left of his wine.

"You hush. We're bonding. You go...tie a ribbon."

Flynn cracked up at Dad's word, just chortling.

"Oh ho. I see how you are. I will do just that." He went back inside to find ribbon for the bikes and found Mom sitting at the bottom of the steps, right where Flynn said she would be. "Go to bed, Mom. It's late."

"You sure? I'm barely keeping my eyes open..."

"I'm sure. Santa is almost done, and then we just have to put things around the tree. Dad is having a great time with Flynn." He helped her up. "Thank you so much."

"I love you. Tomorrow is going to be an amazing day. I can't wait to see the kids' faces when they wake up." She stood and hugged him tight.

He held on just as tight for a second then watched her go. "Merry Christmas, Mom. I love you too."

He needed to find some ribbon. And maybe he'd refill their wine. Why not? It was Christmas.

IT WAS LATE when they crawled into bed, and they were toasty—not drunk, but silly and giggling like children as they snuggled in together in a real, wonderful, comfortable bed.

It didn't even matter that they were at Kiren's folks. Flynn was over the moon, a little horny, and warm.

"Are you feeling all *bonded* with Dad now?" Kiren tugged the covers up over them.

"Oh, yeah. I'm super bondy boy." He snorted at himself, tickled as shit.

Kiren was giggling in the darkness. "If we had gotten divorced he'd have thrown me out and had you over for Christmas dinner."

"We're not getting divorced, though. Not at all."

"Nope. Not now, not ever." Kiren blew a raspberry under his collar bone. "How naughty can we be and still have Santa show up?" Kiren circled a nipple with his tongue. "Never mind, I don't care if there is coal in my stocking. I have you."

"You're better than any present, babe." He dragged his fingers through Kiren's thick hair. "Better than anything to me."

"Good. Then I'm going for very naughty." Kiren pushed his underwear down and let him kick them off, then rolled him over and grabbed his ass. "Mmm. Can't mess up Mom's sheets though."

"No. No, that would be embarrassing." Not that he wouldn't strip all the beds before they left. It was only nice.

Kiren slid down and nipped at his ass. "Yelling too loudly would be too."

"Be good!" That was, at best, a stage whisper. Flynn pulled the covers over his head.

"Nope. Coal in my stocking." Kiren spread his cheeks with a dark chuckle.

"So fucking hot. You make me crazy." He was going to lose his mind.

"Good. I want to make you crazy. I'm not going to let you forget how much you turn me on ever again."

"Swear it." Flynn spread wide, his cock aching, his balls heavy with need.

"I swear. I better than swear." Kiren covered his skin with biting kisses, then bathed his hole with a hot tongue.

He shoved his fist in his mouth, muffling his happy cry.

After that, Kiren didn't let up, teasing his hole and stroking his balls with one hand.

The slick sensation drove a line of need from his ass to the base of his skull, and he couldn't think, he couldn't see.

All he could do was pray this was real.

The ache in his balls was real, the scent of his cock leaking was real, and the fingers that pressed in just a little, but nowhere near enough to give him the burn he was craving were very, very real.

"More," he whispered. "Please, love. I want you. I need you. Please."

He realized that Kiren had planned this when he heard the pop of the lube bottle. Those fingers pulled away but came back cool and slick, and this time they pushed in slowly, giving him a taste of what he really wanted.

He groaned, covering his mouth with his fingers. So fucking perfect. So good.

"You didn't want to get any sleep tonight, did you?" Kiren whispered back, twisting those fingers deeper inside him.

"Uh-uh. I can sleep later. I swear. I can sleep any time."

"Me too." Kiren moved again, and his husband's heavy cock pressed against his hole, nudging gently, asking permission like Kiren always had. Always, even after they were married. Even though he'd never said no. Kiren was always careful with him.

"Please. I need you more than breath." Flynn was more than willing to beg.

"Fuck." He heard Kiren stifle a moan as that cock pushed slowly inside him. "So good. Missed you. Fuck, baby."

"Every day." This was exactly what he'd needed, to feel his lover buried deep inside.

He could feel Kiren holding back, trying not to rush, and it was gratifying that his husband seemed to be losing that battle. So he bore down, squeezing with all his might, and Kiren swallowed back a soft scream.

"Bad. Coal for you too," Kiren said in a slightly strangled voice before rocking into him hard and picking up a steady pace.

"Uh-huh. Coal. Good. All the coal." Did that even make sense?

"So much coal. Fuck, baby." Kiren was a little on the loud side there; hopefully they weren't waking the house up.

He dragged Kiren down into a kiss to shut them both up. Last thing they needed was to wake Cass up now.

"Yeah." Kiren nodded into the kiss and pulled out long enough to let him roll onto his back, then dove back in, hips driving against him. Much better. He could see Kiren's face this way.

Kissing was easier on his neck too.

He grinned, imagining himself explaining how he'd strained himself overnight.

Dad would love that. He could see the grin—*oh fuck*. The only thing he was seeing right now was stars.

His eyes crossed and he gasped on Kiren's skin, seed spraying out of him.

Kiren bit his shoulder to muffle his groan, and it wasn't another few seconds of wild thrusting before Kiren followed him over the edge, sucking in air and letting out with soft grunts.

"Mmm…" The whole world was swaying. It made him feel ten thousand feet tall.

"Uh-huh." Kiren kissed him again, even though neither of them had caught their breath yet. "Crazy and mine."

"All yours. Merry Christmas. Merry Christmas."

"Merry Christmas. Best present I could get this year. The best." Kiren slid away carefully and came back with a washcloth. "Mom's sheets." He grinned and scrubbed them clean enough.

"I'll strip them and the kids' tomorrow. Be a great son-in-law…"

"Brownie points. Mom's going to want us to stay another night. I'll make excuses. I want to take you home."

"I want to go home with you too." He had to think about getting another job and all, but not now.

"I put the tree up, and the house is all decorated. I will admit that I didn't put up that inflatable dancing Santa you like; I put up a Santa in a bathtub instead. He has a rubber duck."

"Well...next year we'll have both in the yard. Together. Ducking and dancing."

"Maybe." Kiren winked at him and climbed back under the covers. "Man, it's so much warmer in this house. That cabin can get cold."

"Yeah. It's not meant for winter use. I was just in a bad space." He was so much better now.

"I hope you're in a better one now. I know I am." Kiren pulled him closer. "The kids were happy to see us I think. Funny how easy going they are."

"They want us to be happy. They want us to be together and a family." Especially Cass.

"They want what we want. Parenting is a lot of pressure sometimes, huh?"

"Tons." He took a soft kiss. "I love you."

"I love you. Merry Christmas. We should get a couple of hours in before the pitter-patter of feet on the stairs wakes the whole house up."

"Mmhmm. I have been charged with making cinnamon roll pancakes. I need sleeps." He chuckled at himself.

"Damn right. It's a tradition." Kiren yawned and he felt his husband relax, sinking into the pillows. "Good night, baby."

"Good night, lover. Thank you for everything."

Kiren nuzzled him and that deep, even breathing started right away. Kiren had always fallen asleep easily.

He cuddled in, snuggling into Kiran's throat. Perfect.

This was perfect.

9

"Grandpa you look like Santa!"

"Santa!" Cassidy echoed her brother and climbed into his father's lap and tugged on his Santa hat. Dad had been wearing that hat on Christmas for as long as he could remember.

Their morning had been chaotic so far. They'd been hauled out of bed by the kids after only a couple of hours of sleep, and now they were excited and loud. Kiren knew he should probably tell them to calm down, rein them in a little with treats or something until they were ready to start opening presents, but he didn't.

He didn't think he was going to have this day, not like this, and he was going to let everyone be as loud and excited about it as they wanted to be.

"Kiren, would you come have a look at the coffee maker? It's making noise but it's not brewing."

"Oh. Sure, Mom. Dad, are you good?"

Dad waved him off. "I am fine. Go help your mother. I know how you are without coffee."

He smiled and followed Mom back into the kitchen

where Flynn was busy gathering ingredients for his pancakes.

This was amazing.

"See? It's sounds like it wants to brew and it just—"

"I got it. Can you maybe give the kids something not-sugary to hold them over a little? They're climbing Dad like a tree."

"Granola bars?"

"Perfect."

He pulled out the filter and set it aside, then started tinkering with the coffee maker.

Flynn was singing with the radio, swaying as he cooked, the scent of cinnamon and caramelized sugar like a drug. There was a happiness in those green eyes, and Kiren drank it up.

He started singing along with Flynn to a rocking version of "I Saw Mommy Kissing Santa Claus" until he found the clog in the coffee machine and cleared it.

"Got it, Mom!" He set the filter back into the machine and started it up.

"I knew you would." She kissed his cheek. "Thank goodness, you know how I am without my coffee."

He laughed. He was just like her that way.

"He is too, Mom. An addict."

Mom rolled her eyes at Flynn. "You have no room to talk."

"Ha!" He laughed. "Thank you, Mom. I need someone on my side. Dad and Flynn spent yesterday *bonding*."

"Your dad likes having someone in his corner. I know you always pick me because I'm your favorite."

"Yes, Mom." He wandered over to her and kissed her cheek. "I adore you. Flynn, your pancakes smell so good."

"My Christmas morning claim to fame..." Flynn's chuckle filled the air.

"I'm going to see if your father wants coffee. Don't burn down my kitchen." Mom winked at him, and headed for the living room.

"I am so tired." He rested his chin on Flynn shoulder. "But I don't care."

"They'll crash at home, and we'll nap." Flynn grinned at him, winked.

"Promise?" He gave Flynn's butt a pat.

"I'll make them both warm milk."

"A Christmas Day nap. Wow." He kissed Flynn's shoulder. "So, what can I do? Warm up the syrup? The table is already set. Are we eating and making the kids wait? Or do you want to keep these warm while we do presents?"

"Let them do their stockings, and then we'll eat? And warm syrup sounds so good."

"It's a plan." Kiran pulled out a small pot and poured the syrup in it. Cold syrup made warm pancakes cold. "Dad is in heaven out there, but the kids are a little wild."

"Oh, I bet. I have t-o-y-s in the stockings and colors too."

"I can spell, you know." He laughed. "I put in chocolate and goofy socks."

"Did you put something in my stocking?"

"Chocolate...flavored lube." That was the truth. But he hadn't had time to buy much, just anything he could sneak during their shopping trip. "I didn't shop for you because of the divorce, so you're going to have to accept a rain check."

"I can do that. I'll make you a list."

"Excellent. They can be New Year's presents." Flynn slipped the last off the pancakes off the griddle, and he helped Flynn clean up a bit before they went back out to the family and the tree.

"Should we do stockings before our pancakes, guys?" Flynn held his arms open for Cassidy, who went flying to him.

"Stockings!"

Jasper didn't wait; he picked up his and sat right down with it.

"Hold on, Jasper. Wait until everyone has theirs."

Jasper sighed. "Okay, but hurry up!"

"Dad." He handed Dad his stocking and made sure Mom had hers. "Mom. Don't be too surprised."

Mom had given him a list, and he'd shared it with Dad.

"I have no idea what you're talking about, son." She rolled her eyes and winked at him. "Zero."

"Oh, me either. I was just saying..." He winked at Mom and reached for Flynn's stocking. "This was already hanging on the mantle when we got here you know."

"Of course. I put it up when I put up all the others." Mom didn't hide her smug look.

"Thank you, Mom. I appreciate it very much." Flynn handed him his own stocking. "For you."

"For me?" He took the stocking and sat with Flynn.

"Now can we?" Jasper was poised and ready to rip wrapping paper open.

"Go for it." He laughed and watched Jasper start digging into his stocking. Mom was helping Cassie.

Flynn kept stealing glances at him, in between taking candy canes and a toothbrush out of his stocking.

"Okay, what's in here?" He grinned at Flynn and reached into his stocking.

His fingers found something hard and slick, round. He pulled it out, finding the wedding ring he'd thrown at Flynn during their last fight.

"Oh." He put it right back on his finger and stared at it,

his chest aching in the best way. He hadn't even thought about his ring, but now that it was back on his finger he realized how wrong it had felt and how right it was now. "Oh, baby." He leaned over and kissed Flynn hard, fingers curling into Flynn's sweatshirt.

"Love you. Marry me." Flynn whispered the words against his lips.

"I do. Merry Christmas," he whispered back.

"I want kisses!" Cass ran to them and stretched her little arms out to hug them both.

"Kisses!" Flynn blew a raspberry on her neck. "Love you!"

"No, Daddy. *Kisses*, not farts!" Her giggle was everything, and her smile was contagious, but Flynn's was even sweeter.

"My turn!" He leaned in to kiss her cheek, but she turned her head last minute, and he got a wet, preschooler kiss instead.

"Oh, a big kiss!" Flynn's laughter shook them both.

"Best kiss ever." Even Dad was laughing, the deep sound low and familiar.

"Merry Christmas." Flynn rubbed their noses together.

He sent Cassie off and admired his hand. "Looks much better now, right?"

"Perfect. It's back where it belongs."

"So are you." He took Flynn's hand.

"Cool flashlight!" Jasper shined it on the ceiling, and it changed colors, then flashed, then made a bunch of different patterns.

"You always find the cool stocking presents." He was the socks, toothpaste, and chocolate Santas guy. Flynn found the toys and the fun stuff.

"I sure try." Flynn's wedding ring was back on his finger as well, and it was just right.

Dad stood, stretching. "I hear there are pancakes?"

"Pancakes!" Cassie ran right to Flynn. "I'm hungry."

"You're always hungry, chica. Always." Flynn lifted her, the other arm wrapping around Kiren's waist. "Come on, son. Let's eat."

"Coming, Daddy!" Jasper fell right in behind them.

"Sit, everybody."

"I am ready for this Christmas tradition." Dad pulled out a chair and sat.

Mom gave Dad a kiss. "I'll get the orange juice."

Kiran fell in behind her. "I'll refill coffee."

"I'll cut up Cass's pancakes and make sure Jasper doesn't eat all the syrup." Flynn grinned at him.

"I'll just sit here and eat!" Dad called, laughing.

He refilled coffee, then helped dish out pancakes while Flynn dealt with the kids. He couldn't have imagined a week ago being so happy.

So settled.

FLYNN WATCHED the Christmas tree lights through heavy lidded eyes. They were gorgeous—bright and packed into the tree. Kiren had always been more patient than him with that sort of thing.

His tree at the apartment was...sketch.

"Whiskey." Kiren handed him a glass with a little whiskey in the bottom, then fell onto the couch beside him. Kiren pointed to the tree lifting a finger away from his glass to point, "That took me forever, and I'm not sure I enjoyed it."

That was easy. "We'll leave it up for a while so we can love it together."

"Keep Christmas here for a while? I like that idea. The more magic the better." Kiren held out his glass. "Cheers."

"Cheers." Flynn sipped his whiskey, the burn making his eyes cross. So nice.

Kiren leaned against him, rested his feet on the coffee table, and crossed his ankles. "Mm. So tomorrow we sleep and play with the kids, and then what? What do you need to do this week?"

"Clean out the apartment so I can not pay rent on the first? Discuss how many shifts I need to pick up over the next five months. Make love fifty times."

"Hmm. Maybe in a different order?" Kiren laughed gently. "We could fuck, then pack, then fuck some more."

"Ooh... You have the best ideas. I knew there was a reason I married you."

"It might be hard with the kids around. I can't ask my parents to watch them for the whole week."

"Shh...we'll just have to be super busy from eight in the evening on..." Flynn teased.

"Ha. So busy. So much to do to you—I mean, with you." Kiren sipped his whiskey. "We can pack like grown-ups."

"Ew. Let's pack like horny teenagers." That was more fun.

"A much better idea!" Kiren sighed, then squinted at the window. "It's snowing. We may be shoveling tomorrow. Again."

"I don't miss shoveling, but we'll make the kids help."

"I feel as though we're doomed to be snowed in this Christmas. At least this time we're all in the same place."

"Yes. And we have electricity and snow plows..."

"And heat." Kiren laughed. "We have heat. This is key because that first naked night was fucking freezing up there."

"Yes. That first night I was in front of the fireplace at least..." Kiren must have been freezing his butt off.

"Worth it." Kiren turned his head and kissed him. "This might be our best Christmas ever in some ways."

"This is the Christmas where I got what I needed, more than anything." Flynn cupped Kiren's jaw. "Hey, I love you."

"I love you too." Kiren gave him a sly look. "And I note that we didn't get coal in our stockings, so Santa must approve."

"No. In fact, you didn't get coal at all..."

"No, I got gold." Kiren held his hand out and wiggled his fingers, admiring his ring. The Christmas tree sparkled behind it. "Don't think I didn't notice that Santa found yours for you too."

"Santa is a smart guy. Brilliant, really." Flynn was a fan.

Kiren sighed and took another sip of his whiskey.

He'd been with Kiren long enough to know what a sigh like that meant. "What's on your mind?" As if he didn't know, it was on his mind too. Their issues couldn't hide behind their Christmas tree.

Kiren paused for a minute. "I'm...glad you're home."

"It would suck if you were having buyer's remorse wouldn't it?" He didn't know what to say.

"No regrets. Zero regrets." Kiren took his hand and kissed it. "But I feel a little like we're playing house here, you know? Like, theory is good but how do we really fix things? Long term."

"I don't know. I mean, I am doing the work to be able to spend more time at home..."

"Is that going to make you happy? I mean, honestly? Because I love that, and the kids will love that, but it's no good if you're miserable."

"Working an eight to five? Getting to know my patients?"

Flynn shook his head. "I want to be able to be the doc. I want to be able to have patients from birth on. I want to deal with little things."

"So, you want to go to med school." Kiren didn't brush it off; he was listening. "Ideally?"

"No. No, being a physician's assistant will be good enough for me." He sipped his whiskey. "I can't do surgery, of course, and whatever clinic I work at will need a supervising MD, but...this is going to be what I need." At least he hoped so. There were no promises.

"Okay." Kiren nodded. "Okay good. So you'll like your work, and we'll have a little more money. That's good."

"We'll have a ton more time. No nights. No weekends. Vacations. Sick leave. The whole thing." That was what he was craving.

"That's going to be amazing. The kids will love it. We'll be able to have dinner together, do Jasper's homework and Cassie's reading. It'll be good." Kiren sat up a little.

"We'll have outings. Date nights. Maybe an evening to watch television together. We'll get to be adults together..." Flynn wanted to not miss everything.

"It's been a while, right?" Kiren's eyes lit up a little. "I might even get to come to bed before midnight."

"I just want to be on your schedule. I need to be able to spend time with you—the kids, yes, but *you*."

"We will. I need that too, I really do. But the kids will take up a lot of our time, that's just how it is for now."

"I know. I know, but—" Kiren didn't understand. Flynn didn't expect hours, just...time.

"But we'll be doing it together." Kiren nodded like he'd heard Flynn's thoughts. "We can hopefully do a lot more together."

"That's why I was so mad. I was doing—I *am* doing this for us. To be together. A family." And Kiren hadn't cared.

Kiren stared at him. "I know you kept telling me that. You were doing it for me, for the kids, asking me if I understood that. I got it. You never needed to raise your voice about it. I felt really guilty about it, but I got it."

Guilty? That didn't make any sense. "Why?"

"Why? Because you were miserable and exhausted, you were on edge all the time like you hated every second of it, and you kept telling me it was all for us. Like it was my fault, or I'd forced you do it."

"What? No! No, I'm tired of the hospital. I hate night shift. I was so jealous of you getting to see the kids, and it was like you didn't care about anything but how much the school cost." And that had made him feel small.

"You weren't bringing in any money, and I was trying to keep us out of debt. I don't make that much, as you know. Teaching alone wasn't going to support the family for long. Of course I was worried about money. I'm still pretty worried about it, but you'll be working again soon, right? So we'll be okay. But that's why I asked you if this was really what you wanted. I don't want to go back to fighting about this stuff."

"I've never said I wouldn't work. I've been pulling shifts, doubles when I can, triples even. I just have to be careful once I start practicals." He could get on the phone in the morning and grab a bunch of shifts between now and when school started.

"Don't do all of that. That we don't need. Catch a few shifts a week until you get the practicals done. We can be careful. I've been managing. We can do it."

"I've been paying for an apartment and utilities. I just

need until June. I am so close to getting this done..." And it was a huge challenge, enough to make him dizzy.

"Can you get out of your lease? That would help."

"Yeah. I'm on month to month. I'll give notice Monday."

"Okay, good. That's some real money right? We can do this. And we stay honest about what's not working, right? From the jump, not a month later. Promise?"

This was the part neither of them was very good at, but they were going to have to get better.

"I do. I'm trying so hard, Kiren. I'm not smart like you are."

Kiren rolled his eyes, and he raised his voice a little. Not in an angry way but in a way that made Flynn blink and listen. "Stop that. Stop. Just because I've read more books than is actually reasonable does not make you not smart. We're not the same; you can't compare us like that. Don't."

"I just... You're so good at school." And he had to fight for every grade.

"I'm a teacher. It's my job to be good at school. You have your years in the service, lives you saved. You're literally a hero."

"I don't feel like it." He wanted to, but he didn't. He felt like a...dude.

"Hmm. No? Have you ever seen the way the kids look at you? The guy who can fix anything? The guy who scares away the monsters at bedtime?" Kiren leaned against him again with a sigh. "The guy who makes everyone in this family feel safe?"

"Good. I won't ever let anyone hurt you again. Not ever." Not even him.

"See? In what world are you not a hero? So what if you can't do what I do? I can't do what you do either. That's why we're good together." Kiren turned and kissed his jaw.

"Book-smart isn't everything. I'm proud of you for what you've accomplished, especially because I know a lot of it wasn't easy for you. You need to own that hero badge."

"I just want to earn it." He lifted Kiren's hand to his lips to kiss it.

"You have. You do. But if you need to earn it even more, I'm totally available." Kiren turned and kissed him. "Any time. Well, anytime as long as the kids are asleep."

He cracked up, trying to keep the noise down so he didn't wake up the kids in question. Kiren laughed too, one hand over his mouth. They locked eyes for a second and that only made it worse.

"Shh—shh." Kiren shook his head. "Oh, God."

He'd never been more in love, and that was saying something.

Kiren knocked back the last sip of his whiskey. "Come on, Chuckles. Take me to bed."

"I have been waiting for this for hours. Absolute hours."

Kiren backed away a few steps. "This present is worth waiting for."

"Love, you've always been worth waiting for."

"Good. Last one to bed is a rotten egg!" Kiren took off for the bedroom at a run.

Flynn snorted, knocked back the last drop of whiskey, and then followed.

There was no choice. This was all he wanted.

10

"Are you about done in there, kiddo? You're looking kind of pruny. I think it's time to get out of the bath."

"Okay, Dad-Mom." Cassidy stood up in the tub and stuck her arms up in the air so Kiren could wrap her up in a towel. He lifted her out of the water and hugged her, then set her on the bathmat to drip a little while he let the water out.

"Hey, babe? Do you have a nightgown for Cassidy?" Flynn had been folding mountains of laundry on their bed. There had to be a nightgown in there somewhere.

"Sure do!" Flynn called back.

"Okay, girlie. Let's get you into a toasty nightgown."

Cassidy nodded, shivering in the cool air.

He dried her off and scooped her up, carrying her to their room. He hadn't even put her down when he heard Jasper running for their bedroom. He could hear those feet on the hardwood floor.

"I need jammies too. I want the Star Wars ones okay?" Jasper jumped up on the bed, nearly toppling the tower of neatly folded clothing Flynn had going.

"Hey! Careful, son!" Flynn reached for the laundry, and overbalanced, whacking Jasper with the tips of his fingers as he went over.

Jasper immediately began to scream. "You hit me!"

"What? Whoa." He dumped Cassidy on the bed and reached out to catch Flynn. "Got you."

"That *hurt*, Daddy." Jasper crossed his arms.

Cassidy started crying for no reason at all.

Flynn's eyes were wide, lips parted in shock. "I'm sorry, kiddo. It so was an accident."

"Nuh-uh! You hit me!"

"Jasper, Daddy didn't hit you on purpose, he was trying to catch the laundry that you almost knocked over. It was an accident." He scooped Cassidy up, hoping that holding her would calm her down. "Sometimes that happens."

"Yep. Especially when I topple over." Flynn was aggravated but using what Kiren always thought of as his 'nurse' face. "I'm sorry I caught you, though. I didn't mean to."

Jasper looked between them, frowning with the strangest little suspicious look on his face. "Why are you two being so nice to each other all of a sudden?"

He shrugged. "We love each other, buddy."

"You didn't love each other before Christmas. You were mad. You threw your phone because Daddy didn't answer."

"Uh. Yes. I did do that because I was mad." He glanced over at Flynn. "You were at the cabin; I was trying to call..." Which is why he'd driven up there in the first place. As it turned out, he wasn't being ignored but at the time, he thought maybe he was.

Flynn started putting clothes away. "Grown-ups fight sometimes, and it's hard, because you feel like you're in the middle, huh?"

"Yeah, and you broke up, and now you're not. What if you fight again? What if you decide to start other families with other kids and leave us behind?" Jasper was beginning to yell, and Cass was crying.

"Don't leave us! We love you!"

"Oh my goodness. Never. Never, ever, ever." He hugged Cass tight. "Even when we were mad at each other, you guys were the most important thing to us. We thought about you all the time. We love you both so much. Nobody is leaving."

"But you did." Jasper stared Flynn. "This is all your fault, because you wanted to go back to school. If you just did that before you had us, we'd be fine!"

Flynn nodded, holding Jasper's gaze. "You're right."

"Hey, Jas. Here's the thing. Life is full of surprises and unexpected things. We can't control everything, right? You know how that feels. Daddy wanted to go back to school so he could spend more time at home with us and not be working all those weird hours when we were sleeping or at school. And what he did was really hard. School is hard, right? Well he had to do school and work and take care of us. It's a lot. But he did it for us." He knew that. Deep down he'd known that all along. Jasper and Cassidy were young; they'd figure all of this out.

"I just want you to be my soccer coach!"

"All right." Flynn didn't come back at Jasper with forceful energy. "I can do that this spring."

Jasper stopped. Blinked. "Cassie too?"

"If Dad-Mom helps, yes."

He didn't know the first thing about soccer, but they'd cross that bridge later. "I'm at school anyway, right?"

"You're at the big kids' school, Dad-Mom." Cassie loved to correct him.

"You are totally right, baby girl. I meant that I have the

same schedule that you guys do, mostly." He added the 'mostly' so she couldn't correct him on that one.

"Oh. Oh, okay. Right. You are a teacher, and Daddy is a nurse."

"Pretty soon Daddy is going to be a physician's assistant, and he'll have regular patients and everything. But that takes work and that's what he's been doing. That, and soccer it sounds like." He smiled at Jasper. The kids had every right to be upset and confused. It was totally understandable. He just wanted them to know he and Flynn were listening.

"I don't like it." Jasper frowned, the full weight of his anger landing on Flynn.

"You don't like what?" Flynn's temper was beginning to flare around the edges, and Kiren could tell that Flynn was fighting to keep it together.

"I don't like any of this. I want you to be normal. Why aren't you normal?" Jasper's voice began to rise.

"What's normal?" Flynn kind of frowned at him. "What is it that you want?"

Jasper's eyes filled with tears. "To be happy. I want you and Dad-Mom to be happy! To have hamburgers and milkshakes, all of us as a family! I want there not to be any more fighting! I want this to be over!"

Flynn simply nodded. "Me too."

"Me too, buddy." He took Flynn's hand and squeezed it. Flynn didn't deserve all of the blame, but that was hard to explain to a kid who only knew Daddy had been very busy. "It's not all Daddy's fault, okay? I'm going to be better too. Come here you guys, we all need hugs."

Cassie pressed in close, but it took Jasper a hot minute to come to him. It took just a breath longer for Flynn to.

He'd expected that from Jasper, but Flynn worried him for a second. He knew what he needed to say to his husband, but it had to wait until the kids weren't around. "Oh, that's better. Isn't that better? We all have big feelings, and that's okay, but at the end of the day, we love each other, right?"

"We do." Flynn kissed the top of Cassie's head. "And big feelings are normal. This is hard, when grown-ups do things and kids have to just adjust."

"You promise you're not going to fight? You promise you're not going to move out again? I hate that apartment." Jasper was quieter now, but still upset.

"We're going to pack the apartment and move back here," Flynn told them all. "And we might fight, but if we do, we're going to work it out. Together."

He was proud of Flynn, this whole conversation had to be tough for him, but he was doing great. He gave everyone one more squeeze. "Okay. It's bedtime. Should we read? Cassie, go pick out a book and climb in bed. I'll be right there." He kissed her forehead.

"Okay!" Cass was gone like a shot.

God, she was so much easier than their little man.

"Jas? You ready for bed?"

"I don't want a book. I'm too big for stories." Jasper slid off the bed, and this time, when the laundry started to lean again, he reached out and steadied it. "But you and Daddy can tuck me in."

"All right. I'll be right in. Do your teeth." Flynn started putting the clothes away again, face still, lips tight.

He gave it a minute, made sure he heard water running so he knew the kids were getting ready for bed, and then he gently took a stack of shirts out of Flynn's hands. "Hey. Look at me, babe. Look right into my eyes."

"What? Did I fuck that up?" Flynn's eyes were a little red already, and the expression there was worried.

"Oh, no, baby." He grabbed Flynn's hand. "You were great. That was hard, and you did great. I just wanted to say that I'm really proud of you."

"Oh." That earned him a shocked expression, but then the most beautiful smile ever.

And a kiss.

The kiss rocked.

He pulled Flynn closer and spun him in a circle, happy that he could still set Flynn's mind at ease despite all of this mess. It had been a while since he'd seen that kind of smile —the sunny one he loved so much.

"I'm so glad I'm home, love." Flynn brushed a soft kiss against the corner of his mouth.

"This is where you belong." He smiled against Flynn's lips. "Let's tuck the kids in, hmm?"

"I'll start with the grumpy boy. You can read to our Cass." Flynn winked at him.

"Ooh. Taking one for the team. Thank you." He bumped hips with Flynn and headed for Cassie's room.

The team was back, baby.

11

The kids were asleep and so was Kiren, but years of working nights had Flynn up and wandering.

So he cleaned a little, did some laundry, ate a sandwich, then curled up on the sofa to watch Dateline.

It was weeks after Christmas, and the tree was still up, so he didn't bother turning on the living room lights. He just turned on the giant multicolor thing and let it glow in the darkness like a nightlight.

His practicals started tomorrow, and it would be four months of rotations—not in the hospital, but he was going to have to pull shifts whenever and wherever he could to add to the budget. He was going to be able to work in the clinic, meet people that would become his patients.

Fuck, he was scared.

"Daddy? What are you doing?" Jasper wandered in looking more awake than he should for the middle of the night and plopped down on the couch next to him. "Are you mad at Dad-Mom again?"

"What? No!" Christ, had he screwed these kids up for

life? "No, son. I just couldn't sleep. I start at the clinic tomorrow, and I'm nervous."

"Oh." Jasper nodded. "I have a math test tomorrow. I'm nervous too. And I have all these *numbers* in my head."

"Right?" Poor baby. He got so stressed out. "So you get me. We both have big days coming."

"Why are you nervous?" Jas looked at him, little face so serious. "Do you want to talk about it?"

Oh, good lord and butter, that was adorable. "Well, it's a new job, and it's the last part of school, so I want to do well, you know?"

Jas patted his knee. "They're going to like you there. You're smart, and you work really hard."

"Oh, thank you. I hope so. You're smart, and you study really hard too. I'm proud at how hard you try." He wasn't going to promise that Jas would do well, but he did know that his son tried.

"You got this. I know you do." Jas seemed very sure. "Can I have a snack?"

"Yeah. You want to share a PB and J?"

"Is there strawberry jelly?"

He leaned in. "There'd better be! Let's raid the kitchen."

"Raid the kitchen!" Jas whispered loudly as he hopped off the couch, likely thinking he was quieter than he was.

"Mmhmm. You grab the bread, and I'll hunt for the jelly." Then they would eat and head back to bed.

"Bread bread bread…" Jas opened the bread drawer to get the loaf. "I got bread."

"I got jelly and milk. Peanut butter?" God, this was fun.

He found the jelly and a knife. Jas found the peanut butter, and they were munching on their midnight snack in no time.

"Does Dad-Mom not get nervous?"

"If he does, he sure doesn't show it, does he? He's used to being in front of people, all the time." He'd seen it, but not often. Kiren was a bit of a bad ass.

"That's pretty cool. I bet he's a good teacher. I hope I'm in his class someday." Jas took a bite of his sandwich and talked while he was chewing. "Wouldn't that be weird?"

"It really would." And it wouldn't happen. He tilted his head. "It would be hard, I think, to let school go then."

Jas shrugged. "Maybe. I still think I'd like it." Jas wouldn't know or care about rules about things like that, and he'd probably change his mind by high school anyway.

They ate and chatted, and Flynn treasured this—the quiet time with his boy child. It was worth both of them losing sleep.

Jas waggled sticky fingers at Flynn when he finished. "All done, Daddy. That was a good snack."

"Let's clean up and head back to bed, hmm? We both have to be up in the morning, and Dad-Mom doesn't want us fussing."

"Yeah. I don't want to be too sleepy for my math test. Do you feel better now?" Jas looked up at him, eyes hopeful.

"I do. Thank you so much. I think I can so sleep." He hugged Jas tight. "Love you, son. You rock."

"Me too." Jas hugged him back. "I love you, Daddy. Sleep well."

"You too. You got this? You're good?" It was so hard to tell.

"I got this." Jas winked at him. "I'm ready to go to bed." He got a little wave and Jas disappeared up the stairs.

He cleaned up the food, washed the dishes, and headed upstairs. He needed to try and get some sleep.

"Coming back to bed, baby?" Kiren rolled over and folded back the covers for him.

"Uh-huh." He slipped in and snuggled close. "Love you."

"Did you have a good talk with Jasper? I started to come find you, but then I heard your voices. Is he okay?" Kiren was toasty under the comforter and wrapped around him.

"Mmhmm. Stressing his test tomorrow. Worried we were fighting. He ate half a sandwich."

"We're not fighting. And you? You're stressing too?" Kiren's hand slid over his abs and tucked under the waist of his pajamas.

"More worried than stressed. Big day tomorrow." Not the biggest day. Not even in the top ten, but a big day.

"Hmm. Well, maybe I can help you relax a little." Kiren's fingers slid lower and wrapped around his cock, squeezing just a little.

"Oh..." His eyes crossed, and his breath caught. "Love."

"That's me. The love who knows how much you like when I trace this fucking sexy vein all the way up to the tip of your thick cock and press my thumb in just so." Kiren's tone was low and dirty.

"Kiren!" His toes curled and his eyes flew open. He hadn't heard his husband sound like that in—years.

"Don't wake the children, darling." Kiren shifted lower and disappeared under the comforter.

"N-no..." He swore he was going to light on fire—boom. No question.

Kiren wasn't gentle, and he didn't tease. He pulled Flynn's pajamas and briefs down just low enough, and then those hot lips were around the head of Flynn's prick, Kiren's tongue driving through the slit.

His leg drew up, cradling Kiren as he chewed on his knuckle to muffle his needy sounds. His balls pulled tight, and he was going from zero to sixty in no time.

And Kiren wasn't slowing down. His cock hit the back of

Kiren's throat, and Kiren swallowed, the pressure stealing his breath for a second.

He humped up, once, twice, and then he was coming, shooting so hard his bones ached.

Flynne was still blinking the stars from his vision when Kiren settled beside him again, whispering to him and kissing his chin. "Mm. If you feel at all uncertain tomorrow, you just remember how fucking hot you are, and that I believe you can do anything. Think you can sleep on that?"

"Uhn." He stared at Kiren. "Wow."

"See? You sound completely brilliant." Kiren laughed and kissed him. "Go to sleep, love. Tomorrow is a big day."

"Love." He felt a little drunk, but he had to admit, he fell asleep in seconds.

When he dreamed, he dreamed about Kiren.

12

"I've got that faculty meeting after school today, don't forget." Kiren was making lunches while Flynn wrestled socks onto Cassie's feet. She hated socks and shoes. It was a struggle every damn day. "Mom's picking up Cass and will meet Jas at the bus, but if your shift runs long give her a call, okay?"

"Will do. It shouldn't. I've got a Zoom call with my advisor here at the house at four thirty, so I'll be a few minutes early. I texted her. Cass, give me your foot." Flynn rolled his eyes, but his husband hadn't looked so healthy in years. Handsome too, in his slacks and button down. "Jasper, don't forget it's library day at school, son!"

"On it, Dad! Do you know where my comb is?"

Flynn shot Kiren a grin. "He knows how to use a comb?"

"I've been working on it." Kiren winked. "Try on top of your dresser, buddy. Oh, shit. Strawberry jelly on my shirt. Be right back!" That figured. He took off up the stairs to find a new shirt.

"I don't want socks!" It was one of their more chaotic

mornings, but Flynn was here to help, and he couldn't stop his smile.

He was less thrilled with the jelly on his shirt, but he ran the stain under some water and left it for later, then pulled a new shirt on as he headed back downstairs.

"Dad-Mom! Can we have pizza for supper tonight?" Jas ran out, backpack filled with library books.

"No. Pizza on Fridays. Tonight is chicken." Jasper could eat pizza every night. To be fair, he could too, but he was sadly old enough to know better. "How are the socks going?"

"The toes are trapped!" Flynn called back. "She's going to turn into a mermaid, any day."

"I'm not a mermaid, Daddy."

"Let's see those feet Sassy Cassie," he said, passing by to go finish lunches.

"Socks!" She said, waggling her feet at him.

"Awesome. Sparkly pink sneakies?"

"Sneakies! Sneakie sneakie sneakies!" She grinned at him. "Did you say pizza for supper?"

"No. I said chicken, girlie. Pizza on Friday." He gave Flynn an amused eyeroll and finished up the sandwiches, then closed up the lunch boxes, setting all four of them on the counter. PB and J for the kids, turkey and cheese for Flynn and for him. He'd added a couple of Oreos to Flynn's just to be cute.

"Ew. Chicken. Chicken chicken bird." She sighed dramatically.

"You like chicken, silly girl," Flynn teased.

"We like pizza better!" Jas chimed in.

"You ready, Jas? You have your eye out for the bus?" He tucked Jasper's lunch into the Iron Man backpack and zipped it up.

"I'm ready!"

"Awesome." He opened the front and peered out through the storm door. The bus had been on time every day since the holiday.

Flynn bundled Cassie into her coat, grabbed his travel cup of coffee, and stole a kiss from Kiren. "I'm going to drop off the girl, and head in to get that paperwork done for Dr. Mills." Flynn was working at the same clinic where he was doing his practicals and would stay there as Dr. Mills's nurse until he began working as a physician's assistant there. It suited his husband to the bone, being settled and sure about where he belonged. "Love you, huh?"

"Love you. Have a good day."

"Love you, Daddy!" Jas hugged Flynn fast and hard.

"Bus! Bye bye, girlie love you!" He opened the door so Jas could run out. "Have fun to today, buddy!"

"Bye Dad-Mom!" He wasn't sure which kid said it first. Everything was happening at once. But a minute later, the house was quiet, and Flynn's truck was backing down the driveway.

And he needed to get his ass to the high school, which thankfully started forty-five minutes later than the elementary school did.

He blinked, looked around, and saw a folded note sitting on the counter with his name on it.

Hey babe,

Just wanted to say thank you, I love you, and have a great day.

I'm so happy.

F.

Well, fuck. He couldn't leave for work yet; his eyes were all misty now. He smiled, so incredibly happy just because Flynn was happy. He was starting to get the hang of this be a better husband thing.

He was extra glad he'd slipped Flynn a few Oreos.

CHICKEN? In the oven.

Homework for Jasper? Done.

Listened about every single thing Cassie had done from the moment she left his sight? Done.

Meeting with his advisor? Successful.

Laundry? Started.

Prep work for tomorrow's patients? Finished.

Flynn was on fire.

"Green beans or broccoli for our green food, y'all?"

Cass said broccoli, and Jas said green beans, and he was just about to negotiate when Kiren came in the door. His husband walked right to him and kissed his cheek, then kept on walking.

"Hi. Suck ass day. I need to—I just need to put all this sh—tuff down and take a breath. I'll be back in a minute, okay?"

"No worries." So, mashed potatoes and green beans it was. "We'll have broccoli next time, okay Jas. Looks like Dad-Mom had a rough day at school, so we'll spoil him."

Cassie nodded, so serious. "We should make dessert. Dad-Mom loves pie."

"There's a cherry pie in the freezer, Daddy," Jasper added. "That would be *so* nice."

"Uh-huh." Rotten children. Still, it wasn't a half-bad idea. "I'm on it."

That and a beer would help.

Tons.

Kiren took a little more than a minute. When he did

come back he had that stress crease in his brow but found a smile for the kids. "How was school, you guys?"

"Good. Got a perfect score on my math test." Jasper held up his test with the gold star on it.

"Daddy's making supper and pie and beer!" Cassie added. "And I shared today and said my ABCs twice."

Kiren gave him a tired but amused look and wandered in his direction. "You're making beer?"

"Not in my skill sets, but I do have a couple of cold ones in the fridge." He winked and kissed the corner of his mouth. "Long day in the trenches?"

"Hold that thought." Kiren held up a finger and looked at Jas. "Nice work on your math test, buddy! High five!"

Jasper grinned broadly and slapped his hand.

"And you said your ABCs twice, Cass? High five."

"*Two* times!" Cass said as she touched her hand to his.

"Okay. My day. I had a stupid faculty meeting. New rules, more work, same money...sound familiar?" Kiren grabbed a beer and handed it to him to open.

"Lord yes. You work your ass off, but you're making a huge difference to those kids." And they both knew it. Flynn was so damn proud.

"The kids matter more than anything. This bureaucracy bullpoop—paperwork, reports, district goals—pisses me off." Kiren took his beer back and took a long drink.

"I hear you." Supper was in progress, and there wasn't anything to do for ten minutes, so he shuffled the kids off for cartoons. "You need me to beat someone? I can. I know how."

Kiren snorted. "I think this time the assholes have you outnumbered."

"Never say so! I have germs from all the patients!" He

laughed and dragged Kiren into a hard, happy kiss. "Welcome home, gorgeous."

Kiren leaned into him. "Thank you. Dinner smells good. I'm sorry I'm a grump."

"You're allowed." He traced lazy circles on Kiren's lower back. "It's just chicken, green beans, and potatoes, but it should be yummy."

"It sounds great to me. Simple is good, makes everyone happy, right?" Kiren leaned against the counter, sipping his beer. "This is a decent attitude adjustment too. How was your call?"

"Good. Good. I'm hitting all my marks. Everyone's happy with my performance. I'm on track." And he was loving it. His life felt like it belonged to him.

"Of course they are. You're brilliant. That sounds like a much better day." Kiren rubbed his forehead. "Ugh. I have a headache."

"You want a Tylenol? A hot shower? A massage? All three?" He leaned close and whispered, "Bonus orgasm?"

"Ooh. If it wasn't a school night, I'd take all three. As it stands, I think Tylenol and a bonus orgasm will do."

"What's a bonus orgasm?" Jasper asked, wandering into the kitchen. "Is dinner ready yet?"

They both stopped, blinking, and Flynn went blank for a second, then the urge to crack up was huge. "I'll check dinner."

"Coward," Kiren whispered as he hid in the oven. "Jasper! How was art class? Aren't you working on a clay thing?"

Ah. Distraction for the win. Go Kiren.

"Art? I didn't have art today."

"No? Well, what did you have today?" Kiren steered

Jasper over to the couch to chat, orgasms—bonus or otherwise—potentially forgotten.

"I had gym. That was cool. We played basketball. I'm really good." Jasper was so confident.

"Are you? I will have to watch you play sometime. Would you rather do that than karate?"

Jasper sounded genuinely interested, and he was pretty sure they were on to something "I can really play basketball instead?"

He listened with half an ear while he pulled out the chicken and potatoes and started the green beans. It was a random, normal, easy patter that felt like heaven.

He checked the pie, threw in the Brown 'n Serves, and grabbed plates.

"Daddy?"

He grinned at Cass. "Yes, ma'am?"

"Can I help?"

"Sure. Want to get the silverware?"

"Sibleware!" Cass opened the drawer. She was just tall enough to grab four forks.

Kiren appeared with an empty beer bottle and gave him a kiss. "Nectar from the gods," Kiren said before tossing the bottle into the recycling. "What can I carry?"

Jasper just took the plates from him. "I got this."

"Pull the rolls out of the oven? I got the green beans."

"Ooh! Rolls!" Cassie did a sweet little butt wiggle.

"Rolls. We all love rolls." Kiren pulled them from the oven and marched out after everyone else, setting the hot foil on a trivet. "Smells good, baby."

"Smells good, baby!" Cass echoed.

"Thank you, thank you." Flynn bowed deep. "I aim to please."

Jasper chuckled. "Daddy, you are kind of a dork."

"All the way, little man."

"Mm. Kind of. Sit, Jasper." Kiren scooped Cassie up and sat her in a chair. "Have we got everything?"

"Rolls, chicken, potatoes, beans. Milk. Pie has another twenty-five minutes. We're golden."

"Pie too?" Kiren laughed. "Oh, some little people got to you, huh?"

"We decided today needed pie." He winked at his husband.

"Ah. That was very kind. Maybe today does need pie." Kiren sat and dished out food to the kids. "Mm. Mashed potatoes. My favorite. Thank you, Daddy."

"You're welcome, Dad-Mom. I'm glad I got off in time to make supper." It made him feel ten feet tall. Like he was contributing here and at work.

Kiren reached over, squeezed his fingers and gave him a smile, then went back to his dinner.

"When is it not Christmas anymore?" Jasper asked, forking up some potatoes.

Kiren didn't hesitate. "Well, I don't know about other houses, but this year, it's still Christmas here."

"Is Santa going to come *again*?" Cassie asked, eyes wide.

"No, he's resting now, but we can have the spirit of Christmas as long as we want it."

"Can he do that?" Jasper asked Flynn.

Flynn wasn't sure Kiren was ever going to take down the tree. "It's our house, buddy. We can do whatever we want, if it doesn't hurt anybody."

Kiren just smiled as he loaded up on mashed potatoes. "Christmas was good to us this year. I'm not ready to let it go yet. Okay?"

"The tree is pretty!" Cass seemed to be on board. "I think we should have it for always."

"Not Halloween," Jasper argued, taking a piece of chicken.

"Halloween tree?" Kiren suggested, not even ironically.

"I want a Halloween-y tree! A purple one with princesses!"

Jasper rolled his eyes. "And blood?"

"No blood!"

"Blood!"

"No blood!"

"Enough." Flynn made sure they heard him without hollering.

"Eat, guys. We can talk about the tree later." Kiren gave him a sly nod.

"More green beans please?" Cassie held her plate out to him.

"Of course." He served them up, buttering half of a roll for her too.

"Ooh. Hand me a roll too, baby." Kiren held his hand out. "Is everyone's homework all done?"

"I don't have homework, silly Dad-Mom!" Cassie cracked up, even as Jasper nodded.

"I read, so I'm done. That means I can play my game for an hour, right?"

"Half an hour, nice try. It's a school night." Kiren gave Jasper the you-know-better look. "And you, Miss Cassie, can always practice your letters."

"I don't want to do that. I do that at my school! A C B D F!"

Flynn was not going to laugh. Not not not.

Kiren literally bit his lips together so he didn't either.

"A B C D E Cassie. Geez." Jasper rolled his eyes. "A B C..."

"A C B!"

Jasper shook his head, but grinned. “Silly girl.”

“I *am*! I am the classy clown!”

The classy clown. He met Kiren’s eyes, and then they started cackling, all four of them just cracking up.

“You so are, Classy Cassie.” Kiren pulled her into his lap and blew a raspberry on her neck, making her squeal.

“Oh, Dad-Mom. I am so happy! I love you and Daddy and Jasper and all of us together, and I need a puppy!”

Oh, lord. He wasn’t in a place to potty train a puppy. Cassie wasn’t all the way trained at night yet.

Kiren glanced at him but was talking to Cassie. “No puppy until summer, okay? Then I can be home to take care of him.”

“A kitty? I like kitties.”

Jasper was watching this like a hawk.

“Dad-Mom and I have to discuss things. Maybe we should plan a family meeting over the weekend.”

“I love that idea. Then Jasper can tell us what he’d like too, and we can figure out what works best. A pet is part of the family, right? Not just something to play with. So we have to be sure we’re doing the right thing.” Kiren reached out and squeezed his leg, and he sat a little taller.

He did love feeling like a good husband.

And watching Kiren be able to relax after a tough day instead of “take even more on those busy shoulders” was gratifying.

All he had to do now was keep the pie from burning, and he was golden.

13

Kiren frowned and rubbed the bridge of his nose. This was going to be another very tight month with the Christmas bills coming in, and Flynn still not working full time. And the damn washer had died this morning, because of course it had. Why should they have one easy month? He'd been playing with the numbers for an hour.

He sighed. He'd figure it out. He wouldn't sleep tonight, but he'd figure it out.

Flynn was beginning to pull hospital shifts again. First there was one a week, then there was a double here, a double there. The upset lines around Flynn's mouth were getting deeper, and the last two counseling sessions had to be rescheduled.

They just needed to get through a few more months, right? And they needed to talk. That was all. He'd get Flynn to sit with him for a bit after this shift, which ended in—he glanced at his watch—oh. It was just ending now.

Great.

It was late, but he hopped up to get a plate put together

for Flynn. Everyone felt better after a meal. Then maybe they could talk.

He started to get up when he caught sight of the pile of essays he still had to read and sighed. He'd spent too long trying to figure out the budget, but it had to be done.

He pulled the stack of papers over and started flipping through them. Something caught his eye, and he pulled the essay out and picked up his trusty red pen.

Before he knew it, he was balls deep into dangling modifiers when the back door opened, and Flynn came in, stomping the snow off his boots.

"Hey, babe."

"Hey, love." Shit. He was supposed to be warming up dinner. He hopped out of his seat and moved toward the kitchen. "Cold out?"

"Yep, but it's not snowing. How's the grading going?" Flynn shrugged off his coat and hung it up, suddenly beginning to cough, deep and hard.

He stopped and turned around, watching Flynn bend over a little with the force of the cough. "Hey. That doesn't sound good." Flynn didn't get sick often.

"Yeah. I tested. It's just a cough. Irritating as fuck though. Grr."

"Are you hungry? I made dinner. I meant to warm a plate up for you before you got home, but I lost track of time." He stuck a hand out and felt Flynn's forehead.

"What did you make?" Flynn was burning up. Dammit.

"Meatloaf and mashed potatoes. Sit." Before kids, he hadn't even owned a thermometer. Now, they had one in every bathroom and one in the junk drawer in the kitchen. He pulled it out and beeped Flynn's forehead.

"I'm fine."

He showed Flynn the thermometer. 101.9.

"Uh-huh. Fine. Mashed potatoes sound amazing." Flynn gave him a wry grin.

"Mashed potatoes and Tylenol." And then he'd put his husband to bed. He put the thermometer away and got out the mashed potatoes. They were easy on the stomach and carbs were good for a cold.

"Oh, you don't have to worry. You are the one that works in a petri dish of teenagers."

"I'm not worried. I don't want the kids sick though, so you're going to our bedroom after you eat." He warmed up a plate of carbs and set it in front of Flynn. He used his mother's recipe, and Flynn was a fan, but he doubted his husband was going to eat much right now. It was worth a shot though.

"Bossy old man." Flynn's voice was rough, but the tease made him smile.

"Bossy. Not old," he teased back and set two Tylenol and a glass of water on the table. It was good that Flynn had a sense of humor, but that didn't stop him from worrying. "Try to eat a little."

"Yeah. It was a long day."

Flynn had worked from seven p.m. last night to eleven p.m. tonight, between the office and the hospital.

"Too long. You can't keep doing that. You just... I don't know. I'll figure this out, but you can't. It's ludicrous."

"I know, but we need the money, so—" Flynn shrugged. "What else can I do?"

"I don't know, babe. I don't know. Get better for starters." He'd tutor after school maybe. Ask his mom to watch the kids. Flynn had given his pound of flesh.

"Yeah. I'll mainline Dayquil and vitamin B tomorrow." Flynn winked at him. "It won't be much longer, I promise."

"I think you should stay home tomorrow and rest." One

day. Flynn could take one day to get better at least. "I don't want you to get worse."

"Oh, love. I can't. I'll wear a mask, but I have to put the hours in, you know? I'll stay away from the patients, but I can't mess this up, not now."

He sighed. He had to wonder if everyone worked as hard as Flynn did. "Okay, but school stuff only. Do not pick up a shift."

"Can we make the bills if I don't?" Flynn looked so fucking exhausted. "I mean, I'm trying hard to help our budget."

"If something needs to be late so that you don't end up a patient instead of a nurse then so be it." That was that. The mortgage was paid this month. The utility bill could wait a week.

"It's going to get better, I promise." Flynn's voice was raspy, bordering on frustrated.

"We'll figure it out. It's only a few more months, right? You can maybe grab an extra shift when you're feeling better. Okay? Does that work? If you're not going to eat, let's get you to bed." Food could wait. He could get Flynn water or tea or something.

"Oh." Flynn frowned down into his potatoes. "I really wanted them, but I'm worn."

"It's okay. I'll clean up. Come on." He offered Flynn a hand up. The longer they sat here, the worse Flynn looked.

"I'm going to jump in the shower. Are you coming to bed too?"

He started to say yes, but did he want what Flynn had? They definitely couldn't both be down with it. "Uh. Maybe? Let me clean up and think about it. Go take your shower."

Flynn sighed, frowned, and nodded. "You can have the bed. I'll take the sofa. You need your rest."

He felt his blood pressure rise. “Would you stop? I’m not the one who’s sick. Jesus, Flynn. I appreciate it, but this isn’t the time to be all gentlemanly. You’re sick. I need you healthy, okay? Take a shower, take some Nyquil, and go to bed.”

“I was just trying to be nice, man. Jesus. I thought that was part of my job?” Flynn growled softly and turned to stomp down the hall.

He sighed and rubbed his forehead. “Sorry.” That wasn’t one of his better moments. “I’m sorry!” He called after Flynn, then dragged his ass back into the kitchen to clean up. He still had an hour of grading to do too. He couldn’t go to bed yet anyway.

Too hot hands landed on the back of his neck, rubbing. “Me too. I don’t ever want to relearn how to sleep without you. Can we both sleep in the living room?”

He snorted, then turned around and gave Flynn a hug. “We’ll sleep together. In bed. Fuck the germs. Why is this so hard?”

“Because we’re exhausted and broke? Because we don’t want to fuck up again? Because we love each other really bad?”

“Really, really bad.” He kissed Flynn’s cheek. It was still burning up. “Okay. You shower, I’ll clean up. I have an hour or so of grading to do, so you can nap on the couch and then we’ll go up to bed together. Deal?”

“Perfect. I’ll take Nyquil before I come back in so you don’t have to hear me gagging over the taste.”

He didn’t point out that taking Nyquil now might make it hard to get him up to bed later. They’d manage. He wanted Flynn to sleep. “I appreciate that because, ew.”

“I totally agree. Love you, hottie.”

"I love you, sicky. Right now, you are definitely hotter than I am." He winked at Flynn and sent him on his way.

Cleaning up wouldn't take him five minutes. He was just going burn everything Flynn had touched.

"COME HAVE A BEER WITH US?" One of the pretty new ER doctors asked, and Flynn shook his head.

He had paperwork to do, kids to love on, and he was coming off another double and heading into a Sunday night with a grumpy husband who just wanted help putting the kids in bed. "I can't. I got to get home."

"It's a bitch, isn't it? Having kids?" Penny swatted his arm as she walked by.

"Every day," he teased back.

Actually, it was one of the few things getting him through all of this.

"You need a break, man. Come have one beer on me. It won't kill you." Gray sat with him, just plopped right down like he wasn't going to take no for an answer. "This can wait."

"No, it can't." He wanted to kiss Cassie goodnight. He wanted to hug Jasper. He wanted to spend an hour with his husband.

Gray sighed. "Do you need help? You look pretty rough. Is it paperwork? I can do it for you."

"I need a break." He shocked himself by damn near bursting into tears, but he was at the end of his rope, and he was scared that he was going to fall.

Hard.

"Hey. This is stressful shit without a family at home. School and work—here of all places? It's hard. I'll tell you what. I will finish your paperwork if you promise to go home, hug your kids, and then get some sleep. And before you protest, you can owe me. I'll call in the favor sometime."

"Seriously, honey." Penny shook her head. "You have to breathe. I know. I have one kid, and she's a teenager. You have two little ones, school, an internship. You are burning yourself up."

"See? Listen to the mother. She knows best." Gray took the pen right out of his hand.

"Go home. Eat. Snuggle babies. Sleep." Penny encouraged him to start moving, heading for his truck, and he stumbled his way over, crawling in and closing his eyes for ten minutes before he headed out.

He woke up to his phone ringing, and he fumbled around for it in the dark. How was it already dark? He didn't find the phone before it stopped ringing, but when he did, he scrolled through his missed calls.

There were four, all from Kiren.

And a line of text messages.

KIREN:

Working late?

Coming home soon?

Hey, pick up. Is everything okay?

Babe?

Flynn please call me

Ok I see your truck is still at the hospital. Would you please call? I'm going to assume you're stuck with an emergency

Ok now I'm worried

CALL ME

"Fuck." He dialed, starting the truck and pulling out of the spot. "Hey, you. Sorry!"

I fell asleep in the truck.

"Flynn. Thank God. Are you coming home? Are you okay?" Kiren sounded frantic. "I was about to call your Dad and—just come home. Are you okay to drive, babe?"

"I am. I'm on the road. I got into the truck and closed my eyes for a second, and it was a hell of a lot longer, I guess."

There was a long pause before Kiren spoke. "You were sleeping? In your truck?"

"I just closed my eyes a second. I came out to head home and—it was just for a second." It was just supposed to be for a second."

"Come home. We'll talk when you get here. Please be careful." There was a sigh before Kiren hung up the phone.

Fuck, he hated starting out in trouble.

Hated it.

Still, he didn't speed—he did sing really loud—but he was safe, and he pulled into the driveway and parked, heading in to take his medicine.

Pun intended.

The door opened before he'd gotten both feet on the ground, and Kiren stood there in the doorway waiting for him. When he reached the door, Kiren stepped out of the way, closed it, and pulled him into a hard hug. "Fuck, I'm so mad at you."

"I'm sorry. I didn't mean to scare you." And he could say that part. "I was just so tired, I guess. I just closed my eyes for a second, but—"

"I know. You're exhausted, and I totally understand; I was just worried. My stomach has been in knots for two hours, and I have a huge headache. You know it's bad when

I seriously consider calling your dad." Kiren hadn't let him go yet.

"Two hours?" Oh fuck. No. No way. "I missed kissing Cass goodnight?"

Kiren let him go. "She's been asleep for ages. But you should go up and kiss her anyway. I promised her you would."

"I will. I'll be right back." He ran up and tucked her back under her covers, kissing her forehead. "Love you, baby girl."

"Daddy."

"That's right." He checked on Jasper, putting Mr. Moo up on the bed next to his son before dropping off his shoes in their bedroom.

Kiren was in the kitchen when he got back warming up a plate for him. "I'm sorry I'm neurotic. I was really hoping to spend some time with you tonight. Sit. I have dinner."

"I was too. I promise. I swear to God, man. I didn't do it on purpose. Let me order us a pizza?" Surely they could afford that...

"I ate, babe. Your dinner is almost ready. We're having pizza with the kids this weekend, okay?" Kiren came to him and kissed his forehead. "But thank you."

"I just—" He was so fucking tired. Everything hurt, and he couldn't keep it together.

He needed to quit whining.

"I made myself work to distract myself, so my grading is almost done. You eat, I'll finish up, and then let's crawl into bed, hm? We can talk until we crash." Kiren set his plate down. More leftover meatloaf, fried potatoes and green beans. He'd seen this meal a lot.

Still, it was better than most everything at the cafeteria, so he'd eat it. "Thank you. It looks good."

"Thanks. Boring, but cheap, and it saves time. The kids love it. That's the end of it though. You might wind up with mac and cheese and hot dogs tomorrow." Kiren's smile was tired. In fact, he hadn't really noticed how worn out Kiren looked until now.

"I'm not working a shift tomorrow, so I can cook." It might still be hot dogs and mac and cheese, but at least Kiren didn't have to cook it. "I think I'm home in the evenings for most the rest of the week."

He'd have to check.

Kiren studied him for a minute. "Let's see how tomorrow goes."

"Okay. Okay, sure. I'm sorry, Kiren. I swear to you, I didn't mean to fall asleep."

"Of course you didn't. I know that. I just...making plans doesn't seem like the best idea right now. I think we're in day-to-day mode."

"Okay. I'm going to figure supper though, okay?"

"Sure. That would be nice. Thank you." Kiren started cleaning up. "Do you want to head up for a shower?"

"With you?" It was worth a shot, right? Just a moment of adult time with his man?

The smile he got this time was less tired and a lot happier. "That sounds like a brilliant idea." Kiren dried his hands and pulled him out of his chair. "Now?"

"Now. Please." He dragged Kiren in and kissed him hard. "I love you."

"I love you." Kiren backed out of the kitchen. "Take me upstairs, babe."

"Take you upstairs. In the shower. On the bed. Wherever you want."

"Fuck, yeah." Kiren took the steps two at a time and tugged his shirt off as he hit the bedroom.

"You are still the finest motherfucker on earth." He had to touch, loving how his hands looked on Kiren's skin.

"I need you, babe. Fuck sleep. This is what I need." Kiren tugged at him, fingers tangling in his shirt.

"I'm yours." He grabbed Kiren's hair and demanded another hard kiss. He was going to remind Kiren why they'd given each other another chance.

Kiren returned the kiss, tongue shoving past his lips asking for even more before Kiren turned and pushed him down onto their bed. The look on Kiren's face was determined as he wrestled Flynn's scrubs down and his briefs along with them.

They weren't going to make it to the shower. Not yet. Maybe for round two, if they were enthusiastic.

He stretched up tall and spread wide, letting Kiren see everything.

"That's my man. Fuck, you're just everything right now." Kiren climbed up between his knees, lips dropping to his chest for a taste, one hand opening the drawer in the bedside table. "Shower next. I want all of you first."

"Works for me. I'm yours. I want you." All the time. He was all Kiren's.

Kiren produced the lube and wasted no time using it. Flynn pulled his knees back and shivered at the first touch of the cool stuff that eased the way for two fingers.

He loved the way Kiren watched him, wanted him, loved him.

Kiren's fingers worked him gently but purposefully. "How much warm up do you need, babe? I'm so ready for you."

"I want you to fuck me. I'm burning up inside." He pulled his knees up higher.

Those fingers disappeared, and Kiren quickly replaced

his hot, hard cock. "You make me ache." Kiren in, giving him a minute to adjust before groaning and sinking so deep no light could pass between them.

"Love you. God, I love you so much." He smashed their mouths together, shutting himself up. The last thing he needed was to wake up one of the kids.

Their kiss was endless, only breaking for gulps of air until they were both sweating and out of their heads, just feeling, giving and taking, working toward making each other fly.

Kiren bit his lips closed and tossed his head back, hips driving hard and sending that cock deep inside him.

Flynn's body convulsed, spunk pouring out of him, heat spraying over his belly as he tightened around Kiren's cock.

Kiren shuddered and went rigid right after him, muffling a cry against his shoulder as more heat filled him. "Love you," Kiren whispered roughly. "Love you so much."

"Thank God." He held on, clinging to his husband, swallowing hard as he focused on the aftershocks buzzing through him.

Kiren slid to his side with a sigh but let him stay close and curled an arm around his back. "Yeah. The rest is just noise. As long as we have this, we have everything, babe. Everything."

"You know it. It's...more than most have, you and me."

"In the half an hour or so that I was worried you were dead in a ditch, I actually thought, how the hell am I going to do this without him?" Kiren huffed out a soft laugh.

"I'm sorry, honey. I swear to you, it wasn't on purpose." And he felt like shit about it.

"Oh, I know, babe. I was just joking, I'm sorry. I was worried, but I never thought you were dead. Honest." Kiren kissed him to make the point. "We're good. You're here. And

I don't have to make mac and cheese tomorrow." The little raspberry Kiren blew on his neck made him feel better. "Shower?"

"Sounds perfect. I'll lather you up, nice and easy, so you're ready to sleep."

"I'm ready for sleep, but somebody's spunk is all over me." Kiren winked and sat up with a groan. "I think I'm creaking though."

"You did a great job, for a creaky guy..." he teased.

"I'm pretty sure I can fully stand up for a whole shower. Are you?" Kiren winked and offered a hand as he slid out of bed.

"Not even close." He winked at Kiren, goosing that sweet butt.

Kiren stepped just out of reach and wiggled it for him, then sauntered away toward the bathroom. "Come on, love. You owe me a lathering."

"I owe you way more than that, lover. Way more."

"Well, this will be a good start, then." Kiren held his hands out to Flynn. "We'll both sleep well."

He nodded. That wasn't a problem. He was going to sleep like a baby.

14

"I'm hungry, Dad-Mom."

"We were good, so we can have dessert right?"

Kiren checked his watch. Flynn had a shift at the hospital so they should make it home first.

"You were both very good. Thank you."

"Was he your too-der?" Cassie asked.

"He is my student. I am his tutor."

"Tutor, like pooter," Jasper sang, stretching out the ooh sound.

Thank goodness they were in the backseat; he could tune them both out a little.

Usually his mom watched the kids after school for an hour while he tutored, and then he'd get everyone home in plenty of time to make dinner, but today Mom had an appointment, and the kids had to be with him. They were both very well behaved, but the session ran long. Flynn's shift ended soon, and there was no dinner.

The problem wasn't dinner. The problem was that he hadn't told Flynn he was—

"Ow!"

"Hey. Hands to yourselves back there, please."

"Jasper is mean!"

"Cassie's a baby."

"I am not!"

They'd been quiet while he tutored, and now they were hungry, and itchy and he really couldn't be mad about it. "Come on guys, just leave each other alone for a few more minutes. We're almost home."

Flynn's truck was in the driveway, shocking the hell out of him. Flynn wasn't due home for another hour or so...

Shit. He sighed. "We're home, guys."

Jasper took off his own seatbelt, then helped Cassie with her car seat. Kiren opened the door for them both to hop out, then grabbed his bag and his lunch cooler as they ran up the driveway.

"Daddy! Daddy, we're home!" Cassie ran up to the door, her feet slapping against the sidewalk. "Did you miss us?"

"Always. You guys are late coming home." Flynn had a vaguely confused expression, but he opened his arms to Cassie.

"I'll explain." He followed the kids inside and set all his stuff down in the foyer. "They're getting hangry though, so dinner first? Sorry if I worried you."

"I made stew and cornbread. Nothing fancy." Flynn nodded to Jasper. "How was Granny?"

"She had to go to the doctor, so we went with Dad-Mom to toodling!" Cassie beamed at Flynn. "We were so good. We colored and didn't say a peep."

He caught Flynn's curious look. "Tutoring. Long story. Dinner sounds great. Let's eat guys." Kiren could tell already this wasn't going to be easy to wait to tell. He hadn't expected Cassie to say something so quickly, but he probably should have.

"Okay, guys. Go wash up. I'll get the bowls filled so the soup can cool." Flynn's spine was stiff, and Kiren knew there was going to be some blowback here.

He wanted to say something just to hold Flynn over, but he couldn't think of anything that wouldn't make this worse, so he just kept his mouth shut. He ran a hand down Flynn's arm as he walked by, headed into the kitchen to help. "Smells good."

"Thanks, babe. I tried to make it taste like yours, but it's a little off, I know."

He smiled at Flynn. "I appreciate that you did it; I wasn't sure what I was going to do for dinner at this hour." Which was his own fault. Flynn had picked up his slack.

"You're tutoring? How many nights a week?"

He sighed and got the milk out for the kids. "I think we should talk about this later, babe."

"Okay…but why?"

"Why?" He shook his head. "Why am I tutoring? Or why didn't I tell you? And can we please talk about this—"

"I have clean hands see?" Cassie came running in, holding her hands up so he could see them.

"You did a good job, girlie. Go sit."

"She was hogging the bathroom." Jasper came in behind her and sat down.

"Who's hungry?" He poured two glasses of milk.

"Me!"

"Me!"

Two bowls of stew landed in front of the kids, the clicking of the dishes sharp. "Be careful, you two. It's hot."

He knew he was in trouble, and Flynn was probably

right to be upset with him, but his reasons were—what? Noble? That was bullshit; it was still a lie.

It was just a couple of months. It was only for a couple of months, and then they would have been fine, and he wouldn't have had to explain it to Flynn.

Cassie started blowing on her bowl. "Hot, hot."

He sat at the table, but he wasn't hungry right now.

Flynn brought the cornbread over, offered him another vaguely hurt, sort of curious glance, but didn't say anything. He just ate.

He got it, but he wasn't going to argue or talk about money in front of the kids. He helped Cassie get through her dinner, then whisked her off to get her a bath and read with her while Flynn got Jasper showered.

It took Flynn a while to get Jasper settled, and when he came in, he grabbed a beer and started the dishes.

"Beer. Good idea." That was the first thing either of them had said to each other since dinner. He got up from the table and opened the fridge, hiding behind it for one more second before the fireworks started.

"Honey? What's going on? Why are you lying to me?"

"I'm doing a little tutoring, that's all." He closed the fridge and opened his beer, and after a good swig, he picked up a dishtowel.

"Okay, but that's not what I asked."

"No. I know." He picked up a pot to dry it and keep his hands busy. "We need the money, you know? But every time I say that you—you pick up another shift."

Flynn glanced at him, lips opening, closing, then opening again. "I—I hate feeling like you have to pick up my slack. I want to be...magical to you, I guess."

"It's not your slack. There is no slack. We're both giving a hundred percent. I'm tutoring because it's another way I can help, and I didn't tell you because you're working hard enough and I knew—there's no room for another shift, but I know that if I asked you to find it, you would."

And there was no way Kiren was ever going to ask.

"That's fair, I guess." All right. That was...reasonable. Surprising, but reasonable. "Yeah, but no lying. No more lying. I don't need that."

"No, and we said that, I know we did. I thought about that a lot, and I wanted to tell you. I guess I thought I was saving you from having to offer. You're doing enough. You've made yourself sick for this family. I can't ask more of you." He felt like he was the one not doing enough. Sure, he wrangled the kids more than Flynn, and he had a full-time job, but—"I want to be doing more. Parenting doesn't bring in money, but tutoring does."

"Just a few more months, lover. If we can hold it together, then Dr. Mack says he'll have me on the payroll the day I pass my test. So mid-May. Because I'm going to pass. I *will*," Flynn said.

He had faith in Flynn. His husband studied hard, took every opportunity to learn more and get his hands on everything. "Of course you'll pass. I have no doubt. Zero. We will hold it together. We are, right? It's a little touch and go, but we're doing it. I'm sorry I didn't tell you about the tutoring. I thought I was doing the right thing, but I get it. Really, I knew all along I should have told you."

"I wish you would have, but I get it, why you didn't. I can fly off the handle, especially when my pride is hurt..."

"You want to take care of us. I love you for that. I do." He took a breath and reached for Flynn's hand. "Forgive me?"

"Always. Forever." Flynn took his hand, twining their

fingers together. “You don’t have to hide from me. I’m working hard on my temper. Super hard.”

He’d noticed. He knew. He was working hard on making sure Flynn felt needed and wanted. He wasn’t ever letting this fall apart again. “Everything you do for us is noticed, babe. I see you. I promise.”

Flynn kissed the corner of his mouth. “Fair enough. Love you, old man. So who are you tutoring?”

“I have three boys. Juniors. All trying to get through pre-calc. They’re not my regular students, I’m not sure I could charge my students.”

“Damn, pre-calc? Scary. Good thing you work with the teacher…” Flynn waggled his eyebrows at Kiren.

“Right?” He snorted. “Oh, you had to see the kids. You’d have been so proud of them. Jasper sat there and read to Cassie, and they sat through a whole, boring hour being quiet. They were so good.”

Flynn beamed. “They’re growing up. I worry that we did that to them, by breaking up, but they’re both good kids at heart.”

“It was tough for them, but maybe they’ve learned that you don’t give up on people you love.”

Oh, that earned him a smile, and it felt so good. “I like that idea. I like it a lot.”

“It does sound better than ‘my dads are idiots’.” He grinned as he picked up his beer again.

“Tell me about it. I love the answers that involve us appearing like smart, clever men.” Flynn clinked their bottles together. “Want to sit on the sofa and watch shitty TV?”

“Yes. Yes, I do. Popcorn?” He got up to make some.

“Ooh… Hell, yes. I’ll get the pillows and blankets all arranged and warm up the remote.”

"Meet you there. Save me a seat, babe." Kiren put the popcorn in the microwave, one eye on Flynn until he'd left the kitchen.

That could have been worse. Much worse. He thought maybe they were finally getting the hang of this marriage thing.

15

Flynn's teeth ground together as Jasper's door slammed, and the temptation to go down the hall and rip the door off its hinges was huge, so he went to the garage.

There he turned his music up loud and focused on not killing his son.

He was fucking exhausted, he had a shift to take tonight, and Kiren was at some school function with his AP class.

Of course this was the day that Jasper decided to be a bleeding asshole.

He felt a tug on his shirt and looked down to find Cassie standing there. He had no idea how long she had been shouting at him, but her little face was practically purple. "Daddy!"

"Sorry! Sorry, what?" He clicked the music off, the sudden silence ringing in his ears.

Fuck.

Cassie covered her ears even though it was quiet now and burst into tears. "It's too loud! I don't like it."

"Sorry, sweetie. I was jamming out." He went for light,

because his temper was threatening to let loose. "You want to have a dance party? I can make it quieter."

"No." She leaned against his leg. "Where is Dad-Mom? I have a tangle." Cassie's curly hair was a constant struggle.

"He's at school for a special thing. Do you want me to try and work it out?" He wasn't her first choice for that, but he was usually able to help without making her cry.

She eyed him critically, sniffing as her tears ended and nodding. "Okay. You can try."

"Let's go sit in your room. I'll get the No More Tears and a comb, okay?" He took her hand and led her back into the house.

"Okay." She held on tight like she was worried he might let go and disappear. They went into her room, and she crawled up on her bed as he found the things he needed. "Jasper's mad."

"I know. Do you know why?" He wasn't above using his kids for information against the other.

"No, he's just mad sometimes. Like you sort of. You're mad too." Cassie just said all of that like it was a simple truth, not a big deal.

"That's true. I have a temper. I'm working on it with Miss Brenda, you know? Just like we all go to talk about our feels." He thought he was doing better too, even though he was so fucking tired.

She nodded. "You're doing good. The music was too loud, but you're doing good."

Well, thank God for that. He didn't want to work this hard and still suck. "Thank you, baby girl. Scoot over, and I'll do your hair."

She scooted and shook out her hair. "Maybe we should ask Jasper why he is angry so we can help make him not angry."

"Maybe. Maybe I'll ask him in private after your hair is done. See if he wants to talk, one-on-one." He settled behind her, kissing the top of her head. "You're an amazing little sister, you know."

"Jasper is a good brother too." She nodded once. That was that. "Be careful like Dad-Mom okay?"

"I promise. I will be even *carefuller*." He wanted to make her laugh.

It worked; she giggled and he could practically hear the eyeroll even though her back was to him. "Daddy!"

"What? I will be the carefulleriest *ever*."

"Carefullerist!" she crowed.

He couldn't wait for her to use it around Kiren so he could watch Kiren's head explode.

"Yes, ma'am. Are you ready for spring to come?" It was coming—not soon enough for him. He wanted to be done with his internship. He wanted his license.

"Yes. I'm bored of the cold. And also spring has flowers and Peeps." She turned her head making him pull accidentally so she turned away again. "Are we going to have an Easter tree? We should put Peeps on it. And Easter eggs."

Where on earth had she come up with that thought? He loved how her mind worked. "Oh, that's a neat idea. We could do that. We could top it with bunny ears."

"That's a good idea, Daddy. You have a good imagerashun." Her shoulders tensed a little as he worked on a bad part of the knot, but he was almost done, and he thought he was doing a pretty damn good job.

"Thank you, lovely. I appreciate that. I like to use my imagination. I like to think about things like going camping and going on a boat across the ocean."

"A boat would be cool. I can swim too, so I would be safe.

And we could see…" He could tell the wheels were turning, but after all that thought she said, "Fish!"

"Yes! Fish and birds and whales. I would like to see a whale, wouldn't you?" He got the tangle out, and he could breathe a little.

"Yes. And a mermaid!" She reached back and felt her hair. "You did it, Daddy!"

"I did! I rock!" He opened his arms, and she pushed in to hug him tight.

"You rock! Love you!"

"I love you, silly billy."

"Can I watch TV?" She gave him those puppy dog eyes. "Please?"

"Yes. Disney Junior?" She could do that while he went to not kill the boy.

"Yes, please." She hopped up and ran for the den, then snuggled under her Little Mermaid blanket. "Disney. Disney. Disney," she chanted at him.

"Yes, Princess. Your wish is my command." He put it on and bowed dramatically before heading to see what the boy child needed.

He knocked once, then opened the door. "Hey, you."

Jasper was sitting cross-legged on his bed, looking at a comic book and he didn't glance up as Flynn walked in.

"You ready to talk?" He made himself not get riled up, because that was ridiculous. Jasper was a little boy. He had bad days.

"Nope." Jasper flipped a page in his comic book.

"Okay. You don't have to. I'm going to go watch TV with Cassie." Little grump.

Jasper sighed. "I just can't tell you because it's mean, okay?"

"Okay. It's tough when you want to be mean, but you don't want to at the same time." He leaned against the doorframe. He just had to wait this out.

"I wasn't mean. What they said was mean about you and Dad-Mom. And you're going to get mad. I was mad."

"Ah. Well, you can tell me, if you want, and maybe we can work it out." He wasn't going to promise not to be mad, but he was going to be calm or else.

Jasper glanced up at him and closed his comic book. "Darren said that you and Dad-Mom weren't real parents."

"Yeah?" Little fucker. "Did he say why?"

Jasper nodded. "Yeah. He said you two can't have babies, so I said that you adopted me and Cassie with a judge and everything, and he said that was stupid, and you're not real parents, and then I yelled that he was wrong and pushed him, and then I got in trouble."

That was a long sentence, but it was more than just words.

"Wow. What a bunch of hooey. Darren sounds like a jerk." He moved toward the bed. "Can I sit?"

Jasper nodded and squinted at him. "Hooey?"

"Nonsense? Baloney?" He lowered his voice. "Bullpoop?"

Jasper gave him a half grin. "Bullpoopy. He is a jerk."

"Sounds like." He sat with his son. "And we wanted you. We chose you. We fought for you, and legally, you're our children. So there. I'm sorry he was nasty, but pushing will always get you in trouble, right? So you have to think about that."

Jasper frowned. "I told him to stop and to leave me alone, but he wouldn't. Mrs. Fry even said it's not his business."

"Huh. Well, maybe I'll have Dad-Mom talk to Mrs. Fry,

teacher to teacher, because that's not fair to you." And if that didn't work, he'd go talk to the little fucker's parents.

"She said Darren was wrong, but she sent me to the principal for pushing him. Would you have pushed him?"

He told the truth, even though he wasn't sure he was supposed to. "When I was your age, probably, and I would have gotten into trouble."

"Okay." Jasper nodded, relaxing a little. "Okay. That's cool. That means I'm like you."

"You so are. Even Cassie says so. You and me, we're cut from the same cloth." And he wasn't going to apologize for that.

Jasper leaned on him. "You and me. That's good. Dad-Mom says it's okay for you to be mad, so it's okay for me too."

"Yeah, but we should talk about it, too, okay? So we can make things good for you. Easier."

"Does talking make you feel better? I think I feel better."

"It does." He nodded. This was something that he understood. "Talking makes me feel less alone, makes me feel like I'm being listened to."

Jasper leaned harder. "You're a good listener. I'll talk to you next time."

"I'd like that. I like talking with you. It makes me feel good inside." And less like murder.

Jasper sat up and smiled at him. "You're my best friend, Daddy."

He was going to die—just die from pure joy. He loved this little boy more than words could express. "Oh, buddy. You are my best friend too. We've got this, you and me. You want to come make popcorn?"

"Yes! And I have math homework. You can help, okay?"

Jasper slid off his bed, and all traces of the angry kid that had slammed his door were gone.

Okay. Go him. Score one for the dad.

He felt about twenty feet tall and bulletproof.

"Let's do this." Flynn grinned and headed out. Math, cartoons, and popcorn—he had this.

16

"So what's the plan for Cassie's birthday?"

Shit. Cassie's birthday.

Fuck.

Kiren glanced up at Flynn and mouthed *Cassie's birthday*. "Oh. Flynn and I were just discussing that, Mom. Let me get back to you, okay?"

Flynn opened his phone and started scrolling.

"Maybe Friday night?" Mom suggested.

"I have to tutor."

"Saturday afternoon then." Mom shot back quickly. "We could go to that bouncy place she likes."

"No, that won't work. Flynn has a shift on Saturday."

"Oh."

He hated when she did that. "Oh?"

"Well, you're both just very busy, is all. And it's her fifth birthday."

He sighed and rolled his eyes for Flynn. "I know which birthday it is, Mom. Can I call you back, please?"

"Why are you tutoring?"

"I...love it," he lied. "You know me, I want to help kids succeed."

There was a long pause. "And Flynn just loves to work shifts again all of a sudden?"

He needed to get her off the phone. "Mom. Let me call you back with the plan. Please."

"Okay, but soon. I want to order her a fancy cake."

Heaven forbid they might want to do the cake. "Soon. Okay? Love you. Bye." He hung up and flopped back on the couch. "Crap."

"Right on. I can stay awake on Sunday afternoon, maybe?" Flynn winked over at him, dark circles under his eyes. "What should we get her?"

"Sunday afternoon." He scrolled through his calendar. "No tutoring. Flynn. *Flynn*. How did we forget this?"

He knew what she wanted. She wanted a puppy. But how would they manage that with their crazy schedules? Maybe a stuffed puppy?

"I only know what day it is because if you don't get up to be at school, I don't have to go to the office, just the hospital."

"We're terrible people." He was kidding, mostly. "She wants a puppy but—" He frowned at Flynn.

"This summer. We'll talk about it this summer. We're not in a puppy space. How about a robot dog?"

"Can we afford a robot dog?" The word *robot* sounded expensive. "Maybe a plushie one with a little doghouse or something."

"There's a soft one with a remote control that barks and stuff. It's twenty-five, I think. She'll love it." Flynn frowned. "Do I need to make food or anything?"

"That sounds perfect. Mom wants—she *suggested*—that

we have her party at the bouncy place. So we can just do pizza."

"Cool." Flynn blinked at him. "They're going to bitch and say we suck as parents, aren't they?"

"I don't know." He sighed. "Mom made some comments about me tutoring and you working. I don't know what she was insinuating. Maybe she does think we suck."

"Maybe we do. I don't know. We're doing the best we can with what we have." Flynn shook his head, growling a little bit.

"We are." He slid over to Flynn and "This is our family, so it doesn't matter what they think." He wasn't sure he entirely believed that, but he needed to right now. "This is about us."

"You know it. Still, I feel like the world's worst dad. Poor little forgotten girl." Flynn winked at him, obviously trying to play.

He went along, because given everything they were doing, it was forgivable. It was far from too late. "The good news is she doesn't know, and Mom just thinks we're idiots, so this will be our little secret."

"Fair enough. I'm sure as shit not going to tell."

Kiren chuckled. "Are you okay with Mom ordering a cake? I can tell her no."

"I think that's amazing. Tell her thank you very much. I'll get my mom to bring birthday plates or something."

"Perfect. I'm going to make a reservation today. Can you talk to some parents tomorrow at drop-off and invite them?" One birthday party coming up.

"Sure. I'll talk to Nan and...what is Kaylei's mom's name? The blonde with the big...personality."

He cracked up. Her *personality* had to be at least a

double-D cup. "Donna. Her daughter doesn't miss anything."

"Donna. Right. She's a sweetheart and a half. She'll definitely show up." Flynn leaned his head back.

"She is and she will." He put a hand on Flynn's chest and studied him for a second. "Want some Tylenol?"

"I probably ought to." Flynn lifted his hand, kissed it in the center of his palm. "Fuck, I'm tired."

"Yeah." He took a deep breath and hauled his ass off the couch to get Flynn some Tylenol and a glass of water. He bent to kiss that tired head of wild hair first, though. "Be right back."

"You don't have to, love. You've got to be friggin' exhausted." Flynn's eyes were closed, lips parted as he began to snore.

He smiled and shook his head. "Mmhmm. And you're asleep, babe." He went to the kitchen and got himself a beer. The kids were in bed, Flynn was out—for the moment anyway—his grading was all done so, he had some time to himself.

He opened his beer and sat at the breakfast bar. Time to himself. What should he do?

What did normal people do with their free time? He'd watch TV, but he didn't even know what was on TV right now. Everyone seemed to be binging something. He was lucky to get ten minutes of a cooking show or a rerun of *Friends*.

He could read a book, but that was a slippery slope. He'd be asleep too in five minutes.

He pulled out his phone and tried to doom-scroll, eyes drooping enough he had to keep blinking to keep them open.

"Dad-Mom? Dad-Mom, there's a monster in my closet!" Cassie's eyes were filled with tears.

"Hmm?" He lifted his head, which had been drooping over his phone. "Oh, hey girlie. Monsters, did you say?" He shook the cobwebs from his head. Those were real tears. "Show me."

She held her arms up to be picked up as soon as he stood. "In the closet. I heard it."

"Okay, let's go look." He scooped her right up because that was what she needed. His whole body felt heavy and with her in his arms he felt like he was walking through a swamp. They trudged up the stairs to her bedroom. "Can we look? Do you want to wait on your bed or look with me?"

"What if it bites us?" she whispered. "What if it's a snake?"

"If it's a snake we'll call Daddy," he whispered back. "He understands snakes. But I don't think a snake likes to be inside, even in a closet. I think you and I can be brave together. What do you think?"

"Okay." She squeezed him tight. "If we die, I love you."

Jesus. Where did that come from?

"I love you too." What else could he say?

He reached for the closet door and opened it slowly. It was dark so he pulled out his phone and turned on the flashlight, shining it everywhere. "Do you see anything?"

"N-no, but Dad-Mom, I heard som—"

A rattling came from the ceiling and Cass screamed, the sound piercing.

A second later he heard Flynn roar, "CASSIE!"

Shit. "I've got her, babe!" He shouted back. God, what an awful scream to wake up to. He'd have panicked too. "It's okay. Well, mostly okay." There was definitely something in the fucking attic.

"Mostly okay?" Flynn hit the bedroom door like a freight train. "What's wrong?"

"Daddy?"

"Back to bed, Jas. Everything is mostly okay."

"Mostly?"

"Go back to bed, Jasper. Cassie is worried about monsters in her closet, it's okay." It wasn't totally a lie. He didn't dare tell the truth while Jasper was standing there.

He moved away from the closet with Cassie clinging to him so tightly he could probably let go and she'd just stay stuck to him.

"Ugh." Jasper sighed. "There are no monsters, Cassie. I *told* you."

"Dad-Mom heard it! It's a monster! It's going to eat us!" Cassie was inconsolable.

He wanted to tell Flynn they had critters in the attic, but they needed to get the kids back to bed first.

"Dad-Mom?" Flynn asked. "Should I go up in the attic, maybe?"

Oh, good man.

He nodded giving Flynn a look that meant there was definitely an issue in the attic. "That sounds like a great idea. How about I put Cassie in our room where there are definitely no monsters?"

"Oh, yay. Sounds like an adventure. Back to sleep, little ones. I will investigate."

"Don't die, Daddy!"

"Not a chance, sugarbutt," Flynn called back.

"Daddy's got this. Jasper, back to bed please. I'll come check on you soon okay?"

"What's in the—"

"Jasper." He gave his son the eyeball. "Bed."

"Night!" Jasper ran for his bedroom.

"Daddy's going to get eaten," Cassie mumbled, face pressed into his neck.

"Nope. Daddy is an expert at this stuff. You wait and see. I'm not worried." He sat on the end of their bed. "Now. Why is our bed magic?"

"No monsters."

"Never. We have a monster proof bed. Go crawl under the covers."

Cassie leapt for the pillows and burrowed under the blankets in a flash.

Okay. He needed gloves. A shovel. Maybe bug spray.

When he got to the garage, the ladder to the attic was down and all he could see were Flynn's socks.

"Babe? What do you need? Do you have a flashlight? Is it racoons? God, I hope it's not racoons. Be careful; they bite. You good?" Jesus. He took a breath. "Sorry. Adrenaline."

"I hope it's not raccoons. They're big, and..." One foot came off the ladder. "Oh! Not raccoons! Squirrel! Big squirrel! Shoo, you motherfucker!"

He rolled his eyes. "Great. Is it just one? Is there a nest? Don't let the asshole bite you." It was rarely just one. And if there was only one, then it had friends that knew how to get in and out too.

"I don't see a nest, but that doesn't mean anything. Whoa! Whoa, back off. I have a water bottle, and I'm not afraid to use it, demon rodent!"

Demon. He snorted. "You tell him, babe! Squirt that nut stashing asshole."

There was a crashing, then Flynn disappeared up into the attic, and about two seconds later the squirrel came flying out into the garage.

"Open the garage door, honey!" Flynn yelled, head and

one arm hanging out of the attic, water bottle squirting wildly. “Hit the button!”

“Shit!” He dove for the button and smashed it, and the garage door creaked open slowly. The squirrel ran around the garage like a maniac at first but took off under the open door a second later. “Score!” he shouted, panting. “You okay?”

“I think so? I...yeah. I have dirt in...my everything’s.”

“Daddy the intrepid monster squirrel hunter needs a shower.” He watched Flynn climb back down the ladder. “Ew. You’re all wet too.”

“I—” Flynn turned to face him, and there were cobwebs everywhere. “Come give Daddy a hug!”

“Fuck no!” He scrambled backward, holding out one hand. “Nope. Be nice to me; that scream went in my left ear, and I may never hear out of it again.”

“I went to fight the monster, though...” Flynn was advancing, making smoochie noises, those pretty eyes dancing.

“You did. And you’re a stud. But you’re a filthy stud and I want nothing do to with you until after your shower.” When Flynn just kept coming he shouted, “I’ll totally blow you when you’re clean, so just stop!”

Flynn stopped, blinked, then started to laugh, his entire body shaking. “Kiren! The kids...”

He froze and held his breath, staring at the door to the garage and listening for feet or tears or small gasps—any sign that the kids were listening. He didn’t hear any. He looked back at Flynn who was doubled over trying to keep quiet.

“Fuck,” he half-whispered and started laughing too, leaning against Flynn’s workbench to steady himself. All of the tension kind of melted away with their laughter, and they were left exhausted, but giggling like fools.

"God, I love you. I wouldn't want to do this with anyone else on earth." Flynn stripped off his filthy shirt, shaking it out a little.

"When I opened the closet door, Cass said 'In case we die, I love you.' Dead serious." He chuckled. "Where does she get this stuff?"

"Her older brother. He was explaining that people who take the last cookie go to hell the other day." Flynn rolled his eyes.

These kids. Every time he thought he'd caught up, they took another leap into something new. "So, what are we going to tell them? We have to get our story straight for Cassie."

They headed into the house, Flynn stripping down to his briefs as they walked. "Well, I told him that one, scaring his sister was wrong, two, no one went to hell for taking the last cookie, and three, scaring his sister was wrong."

"Perfect. But I was talking about the monster, goof. And don't forget, she's in our room. Should we just say, hey, it was a squirrel and studly Daddy scared it away?" They were going to have to call someone to figure out how it got in so there wouldn't be more.

"Oh, yes. Honest is best. It was in the attic. It was just a scared squirrel. Daddy will call pest control in the morning, right?"

"Yes, please. Thank you, Daddy." He made sure that came out just as suggestive as he meant it.

"Butthead. I'll make sure the poor squirrels are safe." Flynn stuck his tongue out at Kiren.

"You're the best. Thank you." He sure wouldn't have gone up there. As the division of labor in the house went, if it needed cleaning or sorting or it was throwing up, that was his job. Busted appliances, critters, and anything involving the basement or the attic was Flynn's. He didn't do cobwebs and rodents.

"Can you put her in her room while I jump in the shower, honey?"

"Sure thing, babe." He hurried ahead so he could move Cassie before Flynn got there. She was out cold and easy to pick up, except that she seemed to weigh three times as much when she was sleeping.

She made a little grunt of protest when he put her down and he kissed her forehead. "Sweet dreams, girlie. Love you."

He didn't get so much as a twitch in return and that was just fine with him.

On the way back he ducked into Jasper's room and tucked him back in. He was doubled over like he'd crashed while waiting to see what they found in the attic.

Okay. Parents one, monsters zero.

Now, he owed a certain wet and brave husband a blowjob. Poor abused him.

He locked the bedroom door and headed into the bathroom.

17

Flynn pulled into a parking lot of the City Market and killed the engine. Then he called his dad, his fingers shaking so hard he almost missed the contact on the screen.

"Hey, you, what's—"

"Dad, I—" Suddenly Flynn couldn't breathe.

"What's wrong? Where are you? Are the kids okay?"

"Uh-huh. Fine. They're fine. I just... I fell asleep driving home, and for a second, I didn't know where I was!" He'd been burning the candle at both ends and in the middle, and he was starting to crack.

"Okay. Where are you right now? Are you pulled over somewhere safe?" Dad was speaking slowly, words measured and careful.

"Yeah. Yeah, I'm at the grocery store. I just had to stop. I scared myself." And he couldn't scare Kiren.

"Good. You did the right thing. Do you want me to come pick you up? Or I can stay on the phone with you until you get home..."

"Just...can we just talk a minute? I just need to know I can do this."

"Can you do it?"

"What?" He couldn't follow.

"Working and interning and being a dad and husband. Can you do all of that?"

"I have to." He didn't have a choice.

"That wasn't my question, kiddo. You just fell asleep at the wheel and could have killed someone. So honestly. Can you do this?"

"What am I supposed to do? I'm so fucking close! I have to pay the damn bills and not kill anybody—no mistakes at the office, at the hospital, at home, on the road! What the fuck am I supposed to do?" He couldn't breathe. He just couldn't.

"Flynn. I want you to listen to me and breathe, kiddo. Listen. You are a good father. Those kids adore you. You're also working very hard for a career that will eventually support your family, and you're good at that too from what I've seen. You're succeeding. You hear me? But no one is a superhero. Not even you. You're human like the rest of us. Sit and breathe and know that you're doing your best. Everyone sees that."

"I don't. I don't see much. I need sleep, Dad. I'm going to lose my mind." He couldn't tell that to Kiren, but his dad? Sure.

"Can we take the kids for the weekend? Your mother would love that. She heard that Kiren's parents had them a couple of weeks ago, and she's jealous. I'll pick them up tomorrow afternoon. Sound good?"

"Let me check with Kiren, but he'll say yes. He's tired too. He could use a break." Oh, thank God. "That would be amazing."

"Okay. Good. I'm glad we could help. Now, I need you to get home safely, so how are you going to do that?"

"I—Can you talk to me? It's ten minutes. That's it." He hated to ask, but he needed to be home safe, more.

"I would be happy to. I love you, and I always have ten minutes for you."

"Thank you. I can't wait to be able to take my test, you know? To be able to do the eight to five thing and bring paperwork home."

"You're going to do great on your test; your mother and I talk about you all the time. We're proud of you, you know. It's in May, you said?"

"Yes, sir. Two months. I can do this. I can. Two months."

"Two months is nothing. You absolutely can manage. You can call me any time, if I can help I will. We say a little prayer for you and Kiren every night, and we know it's working because you two are keeping it together."

"I'm glad. I appreciate it. I love you guys, more than I can say." He sat at the light, waiting for it to change.

"So, did you get those squirrels taken care of? You remember that time we had a whole nest of Steller's jays in our attic?"

"I did. They had to plug up a ton of holes." He chuckled softly, shook his head. "I hadn't thought about those evil jays."

"Those things were homicidal. Remember your uncle Jed and I went up there in football helmets? We still almost lost our eyes." Dad chuckled. "Good times."

"Yeah. The squirrels had Cassie convinced there were monsters in her bedroom." He turned right into their street.

"Poor thing. You need to get her that puppy. Dogs eat monsters. It worked for you and your sister."

"As soon as I'm not working two jobs, Dad. I promise." He pulled into the driveway. "I'm home."

"Good news. I hope you can get some sleep tonight. We'll pick the kids up tomorrow afternoon."

"If Kiren has a problem, I'll text, fair?"

"Of course. I love you, kiddo. Thank you for calling, that was wise. You're a good man." Dad's voice was deep and quiet, and from experience, Flynn understood that meant he was worried.

"I'm trying to be like this amazing guy I know. He'll talk his grown son through an exhausted moment."

"Hmm. My dad was like that." He could hear the smile in Dad's voice. "Goodnight, kiddo."

"Night, Dad. Love you."

"Ditto." He turned the engine off and took a deep breath. It was time to see his family. He could be tired later.

18

Kiren didn't let himself think too hard about how tired he was. Complaining or wishing for a full night's sleep didn't solve anything and just made him feel more frustrated. But yesterday, Flynn had looked like death when he got home—pale, red-eyed—and he was getting thin again, likely from not eating lunch to save money.

His husband was starting to snarl again too, to lose the sparkle and enthusiasm he'd had when they'd left the cabin before the holidays.

He wanted that back. He could deal with long hours, extra work, lack of sleep, money stress—all of that was doable as long as Flynn was happy.

But Flynn wasn't happy, and it hurt Kiren's heart. It hurt him, soul deep.

Flynn was working hard so they would get there, sure, but two months might as well be two years right now. Even two days were daunting.

Hell, even with the kids and Flynn out of this house, his next two hours were spoken for. He had a stack of exams to grade and—

The doorbell rang, dragging him out of his own head and back to reality.

The doorbell? He looked at his watch because he wasn't expecting anyone, then he got up and went for the door.

His parents and Flynn's parents were standing there like a little foursome army.

And they all looked worried.

"What happened?" His chest went tight, and he literally could not breathe. He had to force the words out. "Where are they?"

"Still at McDonalds for the birthday party."

"Okay." What the hell? "But—"

Flynn's mother held up a hand. "Can we come in? We came to talk to you alone."

He took a deep breath and puffed it out heavily, then stepped aside to let them in. "Fu—dge. I thought something had happened."

"Everyone is safe, son."

He needed to know what this was this about. He was worried again. "If this is some weird intervention? I'm totally fine."

"Sort of." Mom walked in and the dads followed along. "And I don't think you are."

Flynn's mother nodded. "And I know Flynn's not. He's looking tired again."

"We're fine." He immediately felt defensive, like he was being ganged up on. They were doing the best they could. "Of course we're tired; we're working and have young children. It's normal. Flynn has a tough job; he's doing a lot. This doesn't require the four horsemen of the apocalypse."

"Nope, and that's what we told the girls, but they wanted to have lunch out, so—"

Flynn's father lived dangerously.

Dad rolled his eyes. "Look this doesn't need to be so dramatic, we're just here to help. This is a gift from the four of us. We love you. We're proud of you. Take it and tell Flynn no more shifts at the hospital."

He was handed a cashier's check for twenty-five thousand dollars.

He stared at the check but didn't take it. "I can't accept that, Dad. That's a lot of money." He liked the idea of it; it definitely would help, but wouldn't Flynn kill him if he took it?

Flynn's mom shrugged. "You don't have a choice. We talked about it, and we all chipped in. You and Flynn are fighting to keep your marriage together, and Flynn's so close. This is just an early piece of your inheritance."

Dad took his hand, put the check in it, then stepped back. "You two work hard. And you've done some hard work on your relationship too. That's admirable, honestly. We want your family to be happy and successful. So, no isn't an option."

Okay, so maybe he would sleep tonight after all.

"I don't know what to—or wait, yes I do. Thank you." He swallowed hard against a sudden lump of emotion in his throat. "Thank you."

"We love you." Mom hugged him tight. "Call Flynn, tell him no more shifts. Focus on this opportunity."

Flynn's mom nodded. "Don't mess it up."

He laughed a little at that, and Flynn's dad did too and pointed a finger at him. "You heard her."

"Oh, don't worry." Kiren let himself smile, trying not to cry and doing it anyway. "I'm really good at telling him what to do."

Flynn's dad chuckled.

"Can we please go to lunch now?" Dad moaned, sounding so abused.

Mom gave him a kiss on his cheek. "We have to go feed these men to make them stop whining. I love you. Get some sleep. Your worry lines are showing." Mom winked at him.

Worry lines? More like worry caverns.

"Yes, Mom." He rolled his eyes and walked them all back to the door. "Thank you, again. This is so much help. It's huge."

"Good. We really want you two to be a success. You belong together, hmm?" Mom kissed his cheek. "Love you. See you for supper Wednesday night?"

"Yes. All of us. See you then." He saw them all out and closed the door slowly behind them. He thought maybe he was in shock or something. He was trembling a little, and he started to laugh. "Holy shit."

He'd said he would call Flynn, so he hunted around for his phone and dialed.

"Hey, babe." The party was loud in the background. "What's up! Do you want anything from McDs?" Flynn asked.

"No. No thank you. Are you coming home soon?" How was he supposed to give Flynn this news over the phone?

"Yeah. We're finishing up here, and I'll be home in half an hour, give or take. I need to get some laundry done..."

"Good. Sure. But uh, call out of your shift tonight, or get a cover or something, okay?"

"What? I thought—what's wrong?"

"Nothing. Just call them. Please, Flynn."

"O-okay..."

"Good. Everything is fine, I promise. Don't worry. I just have some news and I want to give it to you in person." He wanted to show Flynn the check. He wasn't sure he had words.

"All right. I'll be there soon. We're okay?"

"We're good. I love you." Kiren hung up the phone and stared at the check again.

He needed a beer.

FLYNN GOT the kids in the truck and flew home, his mind racing. What the fuck could be important enough that Kiren wanted him to give up a shift?

He had the kids; they were okay—Kiren said everything was fine at home.

So, what was it?

Kiren met him at the door. "Hey, everybody, how was the birthday party?"

"I got a lollipop and bubbles!" Cassie showed it off. He'd insisted that she keep it wrapped up until they got home, and miracle of miracles, she actually had.

Jasper sounded less jazzed about his favors. "I got a Superman mask and bubbles too."

"Awesome, you guys. Go wash your hands, please." Kiren shooed them off. "Hi." Kiren reached into his pocket and handed him a slip of paper. "Here."

"What is it? Did you get a ticket?" That was no big deal.

He opened the paper, blinked, then read it again. "What is this?"

Kiren crossed his arms. "That is your get out of work for free card, courtesy of our collective parents. I was instructed to tell you to stop picking up shifts at the hospital."

"I—" Wait. His—"What? My what? I swear to God, babe. I did not ask for money. I didn't."

"No, I know, and neither did I." Kiren took his hand. "They showed up here when you weren't home on purpose. They just marched in here, all four of them, like that wasn't going to freak me out. They told me that you're looking tired again, and I'm looking worried, and they want you to not have to work so you can concentrate on school. They called it an advance on our inheritance."

"It's twenty-five thousand dollars." He blinked at Kiren. "I—"

He was going to pass out.

"Mmhmm. I know. I tried to say no, but they were not having it." Kiren caught him around the shoulders and sat him in a kitchen chair. "They said they were proud of us, pushed that into my hands, and then they all went out to lunch together."

"I—" No more hospital shifts. He could focus on school. He could devote himself to the clinic. He could be home for supper.

"Daddy?" Cassie's eyes were huge. "Why are you crying? Are you getting 'vorced again?"

"Oh, no, girlie. Come here." Kiren pulled Cassie between them. "Daddy just got good news and, sometimes, people cry when they're happy too."

"Happy cries?"

Flynn nodded and offered her a watery grin. "I just got really good news. I don't have to work at the hospital anymore."

"No more? You get to be here at night?"

"I do!" And focus on school.

Kiren was all smiles, but there were tears in his eyes too. "See? Happy tears. I bet Daddy would like a hug."

Cassie didn't hesitate to throw her arms around Flynn's neck in a choking hug.

He held onto her, squeezing her close. "Love you, baby girl. Everything is good."

He was going to beat his parents. That was an enormous amount of money.

"Everything is good?" Jasper had been hanging back but finally rushed up to hug him too.

"Yep. All good, buddy."

"Cool. Can I have a hot dog?"

"No." Kiren snorted. "You had plenty of food at the party, I'm sure."

"So?" Jasper grinned. "You and Daddy didn't eat. I'll make enough for all of us."

"Hot dogs!" Cassie sang. "Yum."

Kiren looked at him and shrugged. "I can make mac and cheese."

"Maccy cheese!" Cassie bounced.

"She's got to be fixin' to grow." Flynn shook his head. "She ate a burger, fries, chicken nuggets, cake, and ice cream."

"That's how she does it. She fills out a little and then she shoots up."

"Is that a yes, or what?" Jasper asked, hands on his hips.

Kiren laughed. "Oh, all right. Hot dogs and mac and cheese it is." The kids cheered and Jasper went straight for the kitchen. Kiren pointed to the check still in his hand. "So, what do you think of that? Should we cash it before they change their minds?"

"It's life-changing."

It wasn't even the sheer amount. It was the idea that he could finish school. Learn the clinic.

Sleep.

Sleep with Kiren…

"That's…that's exactly what it is. Life-changing. And they

know it. You get to finish school without struggling. We get to spend more time together again." Kiren hugged him. "We have to figure out how to say thank you."

He would graduate. He'd be successful. He'd be that guy who didn't mess up, again.

"Are you okay?" Kiren pulled back enough to look into his eyes. "Should we go help with hot dogs?"

"I'm okay. I'm great. I get to watch TV with you for an hour tonight and go to bed. With you."

"No problem at the hospital?"

"No. I said there was a family emergency when I called in." He'd lied. Like a rug.

"Oh, there totally was. I needed you home to look at that A-S-A-P." Kiren grinned at him and took his hand, then shot him a wink. "I see wieners in my future."

"I see...meatballs." God, he was an idiot. He cracked up, his entire body rolling with it.

Kiren snorted, giggling with him. "You will definitely be seeing those."

"This is real, isn't it? You, me—our future. It's real?" Sometimes he worried that he was going to wake up and find out he was alone.

"Oh, yeah. It's real. There's no way I could dream up the funk on the socks Jasper tossed in his hamper."

His eyes went wide. "Oh my God. When that boy hits puberty, we're going to have to hang a car freshener around his neck."

"I'm dreading it. I'll need gas mask for his laundry. We'll have to drive with the windows down."

"Maybe we can just build him a shed in the back. Like a Haz Mat situation." It was fun to imagine, at any rate.

"Tell him it's a club house."

"I can have a club house?" Jasper didn't miss a beat.

"No. We were, uh. We were not talking about you."

Kiren lied way too well.

"A tree house! Jasper, you can make a tree house like that boy in that book!" Cassie was not helping.

Kiren got out a pot for pasta and a dish to make the mac and cheese in. "That would require a tree, Cass."

Right. They had a lovely back lawn. There were trees, but none on their property.

"How are the hot dogs coming?"

Jasper beamed. "Good, Dad-Mom! I am nukerating them!"

"Keep an eye on them so they don't explode." Kiren didn't even look, he just kept prepping the pasta.

"Ooh...let them 'splode, Jas..." Cassie's eyes were wide.

He took the check and put it away in his wallet. They could go in and deposit it Monday.

In the bank.

God.

He grabbed his phone and texted the family group text.

FLYNN:

You guys are amazing. I love you.
Thank you.

Kiren's father replied quickly.

KDAD:

You are also amazing, and we love you too.

Kiren pulled out his phone to look at the incoming texts, taking a second to reply.

KIREN:

Yeah, thanks for scaring the crap out of me
and then making my whole year. Love you
guys.

MOM:

You're most welcome. K, please feed my son a cheeseburger with some of it, he's too skinny

Kiren's mom added,

KMOM:

Feed him a bacon cheeseburger and onion rings, then a salad. For vitamins.

Kiren laughed and texted back.

KIREN:

All the vitamins mom. You got it. Have a wonderful night.

KMOM:

You too. NIGHT!

Flynn cracked up. She did not understand texting.

Kiren was laughing as he stopped the microwave. "Get some plates, Jasper; these are done. Pour some milk for the kids, babe?"

Cassie was setting the table with napkins and forks.

"I'll get the cheese and mustard too," Flynn said." Hot dogs required mustard and cheese.

"And ketchup. Weirdo that doesn't put ketchup on your hot dogs."

"Ketchup isn't for hot dogs, smoochie-poo." They had been arguing about this for years. It made them both smile.

"You're the worst." Kiren set out a plate of dogs and a plate of buns. "Guess what guys? Daddy was going to have to work tonight but now he doesn't. What should we do with him?"

"Watch TV and play games and snuggle!"

Jasper nodded. "Can we watch *Despicable Me*? I like the Minions."

"You think?" The boy had minion sheets. Curtains.

"It's a plan. I'll make popcorn." Kiren winked at him. "Daddy might fall asleep during the movie, but that's okay, right?"

Cassie shrugged. "We just want to be a family together. All of us."

Her little voice made him smile. "All of us, huh?"

"Yes. Like you said. Kelly's daddy is in the army, and he is never home, so she is sad sometimes. You used to be not home a lot, and I was sad but I amn't anymore, and that's better, K?"

"Yes. This is amazing. I love working daytimes and living here and being your dad and Dad-Mom's husband. I am happy."

"Good." Cassie nodded like that was that and took a big bite of her hot dog.

Kiren mouthed "amn't?" over Cassie's head and grinned.

He waggled his eyebrows. Kiren was the teacher. He was just the glorified medic.

Flynn stopped, frowned, and chewed on that thought. What the hell? He was on his way to be a physician's assistant. He was going to have his own clientele. He was leaving this program with his master's.

He was not a glorified anything.

Everything Kiren had been telling him suddenly sunk in. All the work he'd put in really did mean something.

He was reaping what he sowed.

He found himself sitting a little taller, smiling a little wider.

"You can stay up a little past bedtime tonight, but tomorrow morning is chores and homework, okay?"

"Okay, Dad-Mom."

"Cleaning my room sucks."

Flynn blinked at his daughter. "Cassie!"

"It's true."

Kiren sighed. "True or not, that's not polite. Can you say that more nicely?"

"Cleaning my room sucks, please?"

Flynn snorted, the laughter just bursting out of him.

God, he loved them all.

EPILOGUE

Kiren could smell the grill.

That was one of the best parts of coming up to the cabin. Flynn loved to grill, and he was good at it.

He put his Kindle down and wandered out onto the back deck to see the grill master in action, lingering at the back door for a second just to take it all in.

Flynn was laughing at the kids, who were playing catch while Ranger, their goofy-assed, fuzzy goldendoodle puppy barked and ran between them.

"Daddy! I catched the ball!"

"Daddy, did you see Ranger jump?"

"Daddy, can we have s'mores later?"

"Daddy."

"Daddy."

"Daddy."

Look at his man. Flynn was in absolute heaven. Rested, fed, and surrounded by kids.

And sexy as hell.

He wandered out the door and right to Flynn for a kiss. "What's going on the barbie?"

"I'm making turkey burgers with feta and cranberry for us and hot dogs for the beasts." Flynn kissed him, smiling wide. "It's a beautiful day, huh? I'm so glad we have this break."

Two weeks to give Flynn a break after cramming for his test. Two weeks before Flynn's normal clinic life began in earnest.

"It's the best. We fucking earned this." He kept an arm around Flynn's waist and watched the kids. "They did too."

"They did." Flynn's smile lit the world up, their family finally beginning to reap the benefits of what they'd all sacrificed for.

"Dad-Mom! Dad-Mom, come play with us?" Jasper ran up, their boy filthy from being outside and active and happy.

"You know it." If you were still clean at the end of a summer day up here you were doing something wrong. He gave Flynn another kiss, then let Jasper grab his hand. "What are we playing?"

"Catch. If Ranger gets it, though, he just runs and tries to bury the ball. I thought he was supposed to bring it back."

"We have to train him to bring it back. You know those treats that Daddy bought? That's what they're for." He hadn't trained a dog himself, but Flynn seemed to know what he was doing. He just played with Ranger and did whatever Flynn told him to do. "Ranger needs lots of training, but he's just a new little guy right now."

"He is. He's a baby. Babies get frustrated, remember, buddy?" Flynn had been trying to get the kids to understand that puppies weren't just small dogs.

"Like Cassie when she was a baby. I had to be careful of her head."

"Right? And she wanted to put everything in her mouth, even things that were not good for her. We have to be careful with Ranger too." Jasper was such a smart kid, and he remembered everything. Sometimes to a fault. "He needs to get to know us for a while."

"And he needs to have fun with games so he's not frustrated, right?" Flynn smiled at Jasper, waved them off. "Go play. Lunch in five, okay?"

"Lunch in five! Let's go buddy." Jasper tugged on his arm, and he followed along, glancing back at Flynn one more time to give him a smile.

"Cass! Hot dogs for lunch!"

"Hot dogs for lunch!" Cassie repeated making Ranger bark.

"No hot dogs for dogs," Jasper said seriously.

"Catch, Dad-Mom!"

Her aim was off, and he had to dive for it. He took a roll in the dirt and came up muddy.

"Sorry!"

"I'm good, girlie." He tossed the ball back, right over Ranger's head.

"You're muddy!" Her giggles filled the air.

"He'll wash, baby girl. No worries."

"Catch!" He tossed the ball to Jasper who caught it neatly and tossed it underhand to Cassie. She half caught it, dropped it, then picked it up and cleaned all the dirt of it with her shirt.

"You want the ball, Daddy?"

"Daddy is next to a hot grill. Do you think that's safe?" He asked patiently.

Ah, patience, one of the many things that came back after their parents dropped a fat check on them.

Patience. Sleep. Libido. The ability to think. All those fun extras.

And Flynn's smile. That was the best thing of all.

"No..." Cassie shook her head. "You catch." He did catch it this time without having to get even muddier.

Ranger came bounding over, bouncing on him and stealing the ball as he was about to throw it.

"Ranger! Bring it to me, boy," Jasper begged, and he'd be damned if the dog didn't do it.

"Good job, Jas! Tell him he's a good boy." Kiren glanced over at Flynn and gave him a thumbs up.

Jasper gave Ranger scritches, and Cassie came over to help. There wasn't a single member of his family who wasn't happy right now. It wouldn't be like this every day, but he'd take it for now.

"Come on and wash up, you hooligans. Food is ready, and I'm starving." Flynn smiled over at them, and Kiren saw them – all the reasons that he had thrown the divorce papers in the trash.

"Yay, Daddy!"

"Food!"

"Woof!"

His future was there, in that smile, and Kiren knew it, to the bone.

WANT MORE BA & JODI?

Interested in learning more about BA's cowboys and Jodi's gentlemen? Want free fiction and news? Join our newsletters!

What's Up with Jodi

https://readerlinks.com/l/2317334

Spurs and Shifters

https://lp.constantcontact.com/su/A9CRUzp/baandjulia

Happy Holidays, y'all!

We want to thank you for giving Thawed Out a try. We hope you enjoyed the story.

If you can spare a few minutes to post a review at the retail website where you made your purchase, we'd very much appreciate it!

Don't forget to "like" our Facebook pages and groups to keep up with all the news--new releases, sales announcements, giveaways, sneak peeks-- and of course the rodeo pictures, coffee memes and just general fun. We'd love to have all y'all!

Yeehaw and thanks for reading!

BA & Jodi

ABOUT JODI

JODI takes herself way too seriously and has been known to randomly break out in song. Her queer MCs are imperfect but genuine, stubborn but likable, often kinky, and frequently their own worst enemies. They are characters you can't help but fall in love with while they stumble along the path to their happily ever after. For those looking to get on her good side, Jodi's obsessions include nonfat lattes, basketball (go Celtics!), and tequila any way you pour it.

Website: jodipayne.net

Newsletter: https://readerlinks.com/l/2317334

All Jodi's Social Links: linktr.ee/jodipayne

ABOUT BA

Western to the bone and an unrepentant Daddy's Girl, BA Tortuga spends her days with her hounds and her beloved wife, having mother-daughter dates, and eating Mexican food. When she's not doing that, she's writing. She spends her days off watching rodeo, knitting, and surfing Pinterest in the name of research. Following their own personal joys, BA and Julia heard the call of the high desert and they now live in the New Mexico mountains. BA's personal saviors include her wife, her best friends, and coffee. Lots of coffee. Really good coffee.

Having written everything from fist-fighting cowboys to rural single dads to werewolves, BA does her damnedest to tell the stories of her heart, which is committed to giving everyone their happily ever after. With books ranging from heart-warming stories of found families, to rodeo cowboys that are fighting to make a mark, to fiery passionate love affairs, BA refuses to be pigeon-holed by anyone but the voices in her head.

BA loves to talk to her readers and can be found at http://batortuga.com/ and her newsletter signup link is http://bit.ly/BAJulianews

AVAILABLE FROM JODI & BA

The Cowboy and the Dom Trilogy

First Rodeo, Book One

Razor's Edge, Book Two

No Ghosts, Book Three

The Soldier and the Angel, a Cowboy and Dom Novel

Sin Deep Series

set in The Cowboy and the Dom Universe

Sin Deep

Trouble with Cowboys

East Meets Westerns

(single titles)

Wrecked

Flying Blind

Special Delivery, A Wrecked Holiday Novel

Seeds and Sunshine

Pickup Man

Temptation Ranch

The Merry Everything Series

Window Dressing

Cowboy Protection

Cowboys and Cupcakes

Thawed Out

The Higher Elevation Series

Heart of a Cowboy

Land of Enchantment

Keeping Promises

Bigger Than Us

Home Free

The Triskelion Series

Breaking the Rules

Making a Mark

Making the Rules

Les's Bar Series

Just Dex

Hide Bound

Wholly Trinity

New Tricks

The On the Ranch Series

Tending Tyler

Roped In

Diamonds in the Rough

The Collaborations Series

Refraction

Syncopation

Puzzles Series

Cryptic

Summit Springs Sapphic (F/F) Romance

Christmas Bizarre

Honeymoon in the Cards

Milton Keynes UK
Ingram Content Group UK Ltd.
UKHW021041031224
452078UK00010B/570